VIEW OF KASKASKIA FROM FORT GAGE.

OLD 'KASKIA DAYS

A NOVEL

BY

ELIZABETH HOLBROOK

Kaskaskia: Jesuit mission, founded 1680-86. Under British rule, 1763. A county of Virginia, 1778. Northwestern Territory, 1787. Territory of Indiana, 1802. Territory of Illinois, 1809. State of Illinois, 1818.

CHICAGO:
THE SCHULTE PUBLISHING COMPANY.
1893.

DEDICATION.

To The Illinois Woman's Exposition Board.

A thought that had lain dormant for years was called into activity when one of your number, Frances Welles Shepard, came to us and organized our county. In the development of the Colonial exhibit from Old Kaskaskia, a study of the rich field of village tradition and history caused this thought to take the form of the present work, which is respectfully inscribed to you by

THE AUTHOR.

PREFACE.

"The village of Notre Dame de Cascasquias is by far the most considerable settlement in the country of the Illinois, as well from the number of its inhabitants as from its advantageous situation."—Capt. Pitman in 1766.

WILL the general reader pause for a moment and give attention to a tale whose scenes are located in and around the village which was a hundred years old when the above description was written?

When the question as to the Northwest Territory was agitating the eastern coast, a fair blossom from a seed of civilization dropped in the wilderness long years before was being nurtured, its roots drawing sustenance along the lines of connection sent out to France, to Canada, to New Orleans, and to the Rocky Mountains. But the fair blossom has passed away; the fruit it bore has been harvested.

It is with sadness that we hear the cry from the handful of inhabitants left in the village: "Old 'Kaskia is doomed." The hungry rivers are eating the soil that has been pressed by the feet of the red man, by the Jesuit missionaries, the commandants of the French forts, by the "Long Knife" Virginians, by the brave-hearted pioneers who pushed the frontier beyond them, by noble and disinterested statesmen, by the patriotic Lafayette.

Not alone to the people of Illinois should this spot be of vital interest, for along the ancient trails leading to this center great cities have arisen, and thousands of homes established, throughout other commonwealths.

THE AUTHOR.

1. PARISH RECORDS. 2. CHALICE AND PATEN PRESENTED TO THE CHURCH BY THE KING OF FRANCE. 3. TABLE ON WHICH WAS WRITTEN THE FIRST CONSTITUTION OF ILLINOIS. 4. SIGNATURE OF COL. GEORGE ROGERS CLARKE IN 1778.

OLD 'KASKIA DAYS.

CHAPTER I.

THE OUTLOOK.

"Stay, Marie, let us rest here." And the young speaker sank languidly into a not ungraceful position at the base of an old tree. The flushed face and the basket of large white blossoms of the dogwood showed that some exertion had been put forth on this mild April evening.

Marie assented by dexterously vaulting into a swing of the wild grape-vine, that hung a little high, but her weight brought it within a comfortable distance of the ground.

"Not for long, *ma belle cousine*," she answered, gayly, as her supple form swayed back and forth under the green boughs. "The good papa will start Risden in our search; think you not so, cousine?"

But the large, dark eyes of her companion were fixed absently on the prospect before her.

7

The sun's soft rays were lingering lovingly over the scene. The two rivers were burnished threads; the fields were green with the young grain. In the village gardens the clustered fruit trees were in a pink flush of profuse bloom. The blue of the hills beyond the Mississippi, the old church, the homes of Marie and herself, the slaves loading the flat-boats that were to carry supplies to far-off New Orleans—she was conscious of each detail, yet dreamily so. Suddenly she aroused herself and said abruptly:

"Marie, did Josephine say that Monsieur St. Gemme would return to-night?"

Marie, whose previous remarks had passed unnoticed, had in the meantime given her attention to a robin that was beginning its nest in the branches overhead. She, used to these abrupt transitions, answered simply: "Josephine said that he was expected at vespers."

Annette looked away and asked no more questions.

Marie skipped lightly from the swing, ran rapidly up and down the ruined embankment of the old fort, and finally threw herself down at the feet of Annette, and, gazing shyly into the great, lustrous eyes that were seemingly looking into things unknown, said softly:

"Oh, Annette, you are beautiful this moment."

A swift blush passed over Annette's face at this, and an impatient "Fi donc" was the response.

Marie picked up one of the dogwood blossoms.

"Annette, old Francoise says that poison lurks in this pretty flower."

"I love them," said Annette, passionately, and touched one of the blossoms with a caressing hand. "Poison lurks in many things," she added. "Anyway Francoise is ugly and often cross. I wonder that Col. Menard allows her about his place. I always shiver a little when I go by the tan-bark cot around the corner of the stone spring-house."

"Listen! she was the wife of the chief Ducoign, and Col. Menard is too kind-hearted to send her away. She and Moqua, her grandson, have lived there this great while."

"Col. Menard has a swarm of hangers-on to eat up his substance."

"Ah, but the gardens are lovely—*charmante*," continued Marie, clasping her hands in her ardor, "and the gallery I adore. Ah, the moonlight evenings when one walks and walks back and forth on the long gallery! The sweet perfume of the flowers, rising from the gardens, and the glint of the moon here and there on the river, as we catch it occasionally through the openings in the pecan grove!" Marie gave a sigh of retrospective pleasure.

"Simple, what do you know of moonlight evenings, *mon enfant?*"

"A great deal. I am almost grown. I know that you are sixteen, but am I not fifteen past, and Madame was married, and happily, at—"

A merry peal burst from Annette. The bird that was building flew away in a sad fright. But the grave look returned, and she changed the subject.

"Marie, there are many strange persons coming these days, and a queer assortment, think you not? I like it not altogether; their ways are not our ways."

"Ah, but," said Marie eagerly, "are you not proud to think that they must first come to 'Kaskia? There is no other settlement so prosperous as ours. See the heavily laden boats," waving her hand and looking down upon the nearer river.

"There is St. Louis," began Annette.

Said Marie disdainfully: "St. Louis came to

us for supplies. They are so brusque, so *outre*
—most of them. Since the war with the English,
and those soldiers have discovered how fair a
country is ours, they must needs return. They
call it an earthly paradise, with its genial skies
and luxuriant crops. Do they appear fit resi-
dents for paradise?"

"How far away is Virginia, Annette? I heard
a man the other evening (he wore a soiled uniform) saying that once we were a part of Virginia. Do you believe it?"

"I know not," said Annette, indifferently. "It
must have been long ago."

"France seems nearer to me than any other
land—*la belle France!*" said Marie.

"The dear mamma remains a long time away.
How that tiresome business does vex me. Oh,
mamma!" And the eyes suffused with tears.

"There, there, it will soon pass, *ma chere.*
Think of the beautiful new dress and the slippers, Marie—the slippers that she promised to
bring direct from Paris itself. Ah, think of
that!" And she took the young face between
both hands and kissed it.

"Yes, for the King's ball," said Marie, brightening with the thought. "Hark, there is the

vesper bell! We have stayed too long," said
Annette, rising in haste as the silvery tones
resounded through the valley, softened as heard
across the river.

This, the first bell in the Mississippi Valley,
was the great pride of the village. It had been
presented by the King of France, Louis XV.,
to one of the citizens, Louis Buyatte, to be
given to the infant church. This Louis Buyatte
was related to the nobility, and after emigrating
was very zealous in behalf of the interests of
the Church of the Immaculate Conception.

The two young girls quickly traversed the
steep path leading down Garrison Hill, and, cutting across Col. Menard's place, came out on the
level stretch that bordered the water. As they
passed through the pecan grove they saw the
Colonel moving slowly under the trees. This
grove was the delight of his heart. It took the
place of the park of older countries.

Col. Menard paused in his walk to greet the
two maidens. He made them a courtly bow
and inquired kindly after their respective families.

"Is Madame Dubreil in good health since she
crossed the ocean?"

"Quite in good health, monsieur," answered
Marie politely.

"And Monsieur Beauvais?" turning to Annette.

"Oui, monsieur," she answered distantly.

Col. Menard slightly raised his brows, but said no more. After again bowing to them he resumed his walk.

"*Les petites charmantes,*" he said to himself, "but what is awry with Annette? Stately." And he smiled at the thought. "She will be a queen among women some day. What a noble brow, and hair arranged quite in keeping with her own individual style. Marie is a dear little creature."

Then he straightway forgot the girls as he mused on government questions. He had always been foremost in the issues of the day. He was the president of the Council, and many of its wise enactments had originated with him. The Northern settlements were prospering. Everything pointed toward the merging of the Territory into a State, and in his mind the outlines of a suitable constitution were taking shape.

In a very short time Annette and Marie were on the bank of the Kaskaskia. Risden was waiting in a canoe to carry them to the other shore.

The laborers had departed. Some little

blacks were playing hide and seek among the various bulky masses piled, at irregular intervals, along the edge of the river.

As the girls proceeded along the main street, cheerful greetings met them on all sides.

A happy and pleasure-loving people! Room was abundant, yet the streets were narrow enough for social housewives to chat across the intervening space.

A genial climate, fertile soil, abundant crops, and numerous land grants had developed much wealth in the community, but the houses were primitive for the most part, an inter-mixture of luxury with rude accompaniments.

Turning a corner, they passed a horseman, who waved his cap in the air, and they smiled upon him.

A dull flush came into Annette's pale complexion.

"Ah!" said Marie, "there is Monsieur St. Gemme. I wonder what news he bears."

"Adieu, Marie, our half holiday is over. I shall see you at lessons to-morrow?"

"Oui, oui," answered Marie, drawing down the corners of her mouth.

CHAPTER II.

EARLY the next day, Annette passed through the house carolling a gay French song. Her spirits, this morning, were joyous, care-free, whatever might have been her mood the previous day.

Her fit of abstraction and gloom of manner had vanished, and she was as light of heart and happy as a girl of her years ought to be.

She peeped into the dining-room and then went into the garden to pluck a posy to grace the meal. Her father liked these delicate finishing-touches.

Monsieur Beauvais, when left a widower at Annette's birth, had hoped for nothing from the future. His only thought had been to get as far away as possible from scenes that had witnessed what had been a heaven on earth, but were purgatory after the death of his young wife. Hence he had gathered some odd lots of

15

furniture, with no apparent choice in their
selection, and with his two children emigrated
to America.   Of independent fortune, he followed his own promptings in the matter.

Touching at New Orleans, but remembering
that a friend, with whom he had in the past
corresponded in a desultory manner, lived in the
wilds of the mid-continent, he resolved to reach
this friend and find a home at the same place.

Accordingly he embarked family and goods
upon a flat-boat, and then began the long,
tedious up-river voyage, by means of the cordelle.

Annette was a child of two years at that time,
and her brother Antoine a bright, restless child
of five.   An old servant, ever faithful to the
Beauvais, watched over the little Annette.
Babette, the nurse, had long since closed her
eyes upon this world.

Black Rose held full sway over the estab-
lishment.   Her cooking was good, but she was
given to tantrums.   She had been an indentured
servant, but was in possession of free papers at
this date.   However, she refused to leave the
family and would hear of no change.

The preparations for the meal were simple.

The cloth was white, the service old-fashioned, brought from France. The table was made from two; one side of either being round, and the other square. The two square sides, being joined, made a single piece. Two or three good articles of furniture were in the room, one an ancient sideboard of rich mahogany. When a child, Annette had been fascinated with the feet, which represented lions' paws. She would poke her own fat fingers in and around these, occasionally trying her teeth on them by way of change.

But Annette returned to the room, and, placing the flowers by her father's plate, waited rather impatiently.

In a few moments black Rose entered with a plate of hot cakes in one hand and a bowl of honey in the other.

"Good morning, ma'm'selle. Fresh fish for you dis morning."

"Ah, Antoine has been out—so early?"

"Antoine will answer for himself," said a handsome youth, as he stepped lightly inside the door, and, taking his sister by both ears, kissed first one cheek and then the other.

"Antoine, you have too much *frivolité.*"

"Oui, oui, Annette," repeating his previous action with much *sang froid.*

"Antoine," said Annette, laughing, "call papa. I cannot wait longer. Fresh fish—such a change! We do not have it oftener than three times a week since Antoine turned angler."

"Thanking me—do not forget to put that in," said Antoine.

"Thanking Antoine," she said mockingly.

But her countenance changed instantly. A swift expression crossed her eyes—what is it?—apprehension, fear, pain?—as her father opened a side door and entered abruptly.

"Good morning, papa," the two young voices said in concert.

Papa Beauvais nodded kindly to his children, and then all seated themselves around the board.

Monsieur, a slight, dark man, appeared to be much older than he really was. His hair was growing thin, and was well sprinkled with gray. The neighbors usually referred to him as the "old monsieur," though he did not deserve the title on account of age. An intellectual face, but there was a dull look about the eyes. His books, his garden, his large plantation on the other river filled his time. He paid very little

attention to the training of his children. The
early French were neglectful in respect to education. What Antoine had procured of knowledge
was due to the priest. Annette had fared worse,
but at present she and Marie were reading with
an English lady and taking some instruction in
drawing.

"Annette," said Monsieur, "where did you and
Marie walk, yesterday?"

"Over on Garrison Hill, by the old fort, papa,"
answered Annette, looking surprised, as her
father seldom manifested any interest in her
pursuits.

"That was rather far, was it not?"

"Yes, but there are many wild flowers, and, oh,
papa, you should see the dogwood. It is one
mass of white," exclaimed Annette enthusiast·
ically.

"There is a fine prospect from the hill. I
wonder what Col. Clarke would have said had
any one told him to what we would grow. He
could not have laughed in his sleeve at us at this
stage," said Antoine.

"Did he laugh because of the small village,
Antoine?"

"Oh, do you not know how the story goes,

Annette? That he marched his band across the wilderness and took the fort by surprise?"

"That was one fourth of July," said Monsieur.

"It was sharp of him, though, to march his twenty men round and round the fort, so as to make the villagers believe that he had a large force at his command."

"The bluff is steep and the path narrow, even at this day," said Annette.

"The villagers were nearly dead with fright," said Antoine, laughing. "They rushed to and fro and thought that he would give them no quarter. It is thought that the priest himself turned pale."

"Good Father Gibeault?" asked Annette.

"Listen, Antoine," said Monsieur. "Clarke was a young man of twenty-five when he formed the design of relieving the Western frontier. To do this was really to gain an empire in extent. I heard the old men talking about it when I first reached 'Kaskia. The British posts were supplying the Indians with the means of murdering unprotected families, and were paying gold for their scalps."

"Oh, papa!" said Annette, with a shudder.

"Garrison Hill was one of the posts," said

Antoine, shrugging his shoulders. "The French had been led to believe that the Virginians, called 'Long Knives' by the Indians, were monsters of cruelty. Gov. Patrick Henry signed secret instructions for Clarke to march to Kaskaskia. He was a brilliant soldier, in open warfare or in the *ruse de guerre*. But the men and supplies promised him failed when he reached the banks of the Kaskaskia. Only one hundred and fifty men composed the force. And there on its banks at midnight he addressed the brave warriors." And Antoine sprang to his feet and in pantomime represented Clarke in the act of speaking.

"There, Antoine," said his father, "sit down and finish your breakfast. It is enough to know that he told them that they were fighting for their own wives and children, although so far from them; that it was the fourth of July and they must act so as to honor it; that the fort and town must be taken."

"And how was that, papa?" asked Annette.

She had heard the tale of the capture over and over again, but now asked him to repeat it because she enjoyed the reminiscences.

"There were three divisions; two were to

enter the town at the extreme ends.   The third
was to remain at the east side, and capture Fort
Gage.   Clarke was with that division.   The
French in the village were awakened by the most
hideous yells and noises.   They were made to
believe that a large army of the 'Long Knives'
were coming to destroy the place.   They sur-
rendered all guns and means of defense.   The
daylight, revealing the ragged, unkempt, soiled
and hence wild-looking men, made them more
alarmed than ever.   Kenton led the band into
the fort in the meantime.   A Pennsylvanian '
opened to them.   Had he proved treacherous,
imagine the condition of these men, hemmed in
in the midst of an armed garrison.   Gov. Rocheblave was awakened by Kenton placing his hand
on his shoulder."

"Rocheblave was insolent afterwards, and
Col. Clarke put him in chains, did he not?"
asked Antoine.

"And Madame Rocheblave concealed and destroyed valuable public documents," said
Annette.

"Fort Gage was built of large square timbers,
and was an oblong, 200 by 291 feet.   The magazine of stores was a stone building inside of the
fort."

"Did they fire on us from the fort?"

"On us?" repeated Antoine.

"Oh, my meaning you know—on dear old 'Kaskia?" said Annette.

"Yes, a few shots from the cannon. There is a hole in the wall of one house, from a shell. Clarke pretended that he would give them no quarter. The priest and the elder men waited upon him, to know their fate. He kept them for a few days in suspense, until they were at the highest pitch of excitement. Then he addressed them:

"'Do you mistake us for savages? My country disdains to make war upon helpless innocence. To prevent the horrors of Indian butchery on our own wives and children, we have taken up arms and penetrated to this stronghold of Indian and British barbarity, and not for despicable plunder. The King of France has united his powerful arms with those of America, and the contest will soon be ended. The people of 'Kaskia may side with either party. To verify my words, go and tell your people to do as they please, without any danger from me.'

"And the bell did ring, and husbands ran to tell their wives, and all were filled with extravagant joy.

"Virginia in 1778 formed the Illinois country, now a county of that name. Col. Clarke was appointed military commander, and many of the Illinois French entered in his campaigns, and no better soldiers or braver could be found.

"But, Annette, many of the leading men in our territory were volunteers in Clarke's company, which took Fort Gage. They liked our country and returned as pioneers."

LAND OFFICE.

KASKASKIA, ILLINOIS.

CAIRO BANK.

CHAPTER III.

STRATEGY.

"Papa, it was but yesterday that Marie asked me about our belonging to Virginia," said Annette.

These recitals of war and incidents were general with the villagers in those early days. The hunt, the chase, the various Indian wars, the war of 1812—such topics filled up the hours that in the present day would be devoted to the papers or the latest books.

"It is forty years ago, but one," said Monsieur Beauvais, "since Col. Clarke's expedition."

"You were in a French school at that time, Papa Beauvais."

"Ah, yes, I never saw this country until I brought you here, my child," said Monsieur sadly.

"Ah, I forgot," said Annette softly, and the subject was not resumed.

Black Rose startled them from a reverie into

which each had fallen. Putting her head in the window, which stood open, the sash swinging back on its hinges according to French fashion, she said:

"Monsieur, dat yaller French nigger Jule is hyar wid a pack of letters and papers, and he say dat Monsieur get him to bring dem hyah, and he says, dat nigger says, dat a boat cum up de ribber from away down dere, and Jule *parley voo*!"

"Now, Rose," said Monsieur, "tell Jule to deliver his own message," for when Rose dropped into French it was high time to recall her. She had been brought to the village by an English family from Virginia. She wouldn't or couldn't learn the other language to any degree, although it was common for many of the blacks to talk French, English and Indian. She had picked up French terms, but could not compete "wid dem yaller niggers," as she called them in scorn.

Jule gave a very profound bow to the young ma'm'selle as he entered.

"So Monsieur St. Gemme is at home again?"

"He is, indeed, monsieur (with a bow), and glad enough we are. He sends his compliments, he do, to you all, and hopes to have the pleasure of calling this evening providing it suits you, Monsieur," said Jule glibly in French.

Monsieur Beauvais replied that it would afford him great pleasure to have Monsieur call.

"Much of a cargo in last night, Jule?" asked Antoine.

"Oui, Monsieur Antoine. Menard have a fine lot of goods from Orleans. Great dresses at the ball certain."

"Why, I thought their goods came from the East, Jule?" said Monsieur Beauvais.

Jule hung his head; he liked to draw on his imagination.

"Mabbe it was provisions, then. Yes, it must have been that, certain. The ball dresses came from Baltimore, perhaps."

"Anyway," said Jule brightening, "Gen. Edgar send a lot of his flour down next time. I'm sure of that, for I saw the men loading yesterday."

"Who goes with it this time?"

"Francis Menard himself talks a little of it," said Jule as he was departing upon Monsieur Beauvais dismissing him.

Jule loved to spread the news. If he could astonish any one, he was happy.

"Come," said Monsieur Beauvais, rising from

the table, "let us see what this package contains."

He was now buried in his letters, while Antoine and Annette examined their share.

In a package for the latter were silk mits, some ribbons and laces, sent her by far-away cousins; also a ring set with a ruby and pearls, this from her grandmother. Antoine gave an exclamation of pleasure, in which Annette joined, when she saw him open a music roll, with score for violin exposed. They exchanged meaning glances, and Antoine wielded an imaginary bow, and held in place the corresponding instrument.

"La Fille du Regiment, Beatrice Di Tenda, Il Desidero, Lucia di Lammermoor, and a host of others," he whispered delightedly.

"Come up to the attic presently, and we will try them together," she said in a low tone.

"Antoine," said her father, looking up, "I have some letters on business here, and I am under the necessity of going over to the plantation in consequence. Will you see that Risden has my pony ready in an hour?"

"Oui, papa." "Just our chance," he said to his sister, as he passed her chair.

She smiled and nodded assent.

The prospect of a ride on this fine spring

morning brightened even Papa Beauvais' dull
eyes as he came down the walk and mounted his
French pony.

"Yes," he continued, his line of thought suggested by the conversation of the morning, "they
reproach us and say that we have little ambition
or enterprise in our nature, but we make valiant
soldiers, never quailing in the bloodiest carnage.
We will march to the mouth of the cannon un-
flinchingly. They cannot deny our bravery.
Clarke found that out afterwards in his campaign. But it is a vast wilderness yet," he re-
flected, raising his eyes to the bluffs on the east
side of the river, where Garrison Hill stood out
in relief. He pictured to himself the scenes that
had transpired on that historical spot—the
French commandants that had come, and in
time had disappeared; the British garrisons that
had held the fort. "Illinois French they have
named us."

His thoughts ran on, and then he turned his
eyes in the direction of the Indian lodges, from
which the blue smoke was curling to the skies.
A remnant as compared with the tribes of the
Illinois that roamed these forests. A thought
thrilled him just then and stirred the calm of his

nature. The Jesuit fathers crowded out too, alas! and others. The brave Morest enduring the most severe exposure, following in the wake of the gentle and eloquent Pinet. The pious Mermet, undergoing trial and hardship, peril and suffering, to plant the Church. "It is inevitable. They are already at our heels. Is he destined to supplant the 'Illinois French'?"

CHAPTER IV.

THE ATTIC CHAMBER.

"ANNETTE," said Antoine, "come, now is our opportunity." Gathering up the roll of music, he started around the house, and mounted an outside stairway leading to an attic over an ell at the north end.

Annette was nothing loth to follow. The light in the attic was dim as it penetrated the dirty panes of two small dormer windows. Yet it was sufficient for young eyes. Antoine opened a violin case lying on the top of an old chest, and, taking out the instrument, commenced to finger the strings lovingly.

"Who shall begin?" said he.

"You, Antoine," said Annette, restraining her impatience. Seating herself on the edge of a dilapidated chair, she listened with keen enjoyment to the strains of "Lucretia Borgia" and other airs as Antoine tried one after another.

"Now, Annette, it is your turn." She sprang

31

up with alacrity, reaching for the violin and music, which she placed in position.

She made a most interesting picture, standing there in the unconscious grace of a posture that might be envied by pupils of a most artistic training. A white hand and perfectly turned wrist, raised in the act of bowing, the taper fingers of the other hand pressing the frets. The usually pale countenance was flushed with the pleasing excitement of a new score, and the dark eyes luminous with feeling.

Antoine looked on in sympathetic appreciation, for was she not his own pupil? The brother and sister were comrades in every sense. When Annette teased him to let her play too, he at first said:

"Nonsense; the violin is not for girls. What would people think to see you with one in your hands?"

"I care not what they think. Other girls have been known to play. Anyway, they needn't see me, if I only, I myself, can play for myself."

So the attic was the rendezvous, and no one any the wiser, save black Rose.

But Antoine did think it a great pity after all that so much good playing was lost to their friends.

"Oh, Antoine, here are some duos for first and second violin," she cried as she turned over the pages.

"Wait a moment," said Antoine. He flew out of the door and was back in a short space of time, for he had run the block and borrowed a friend's instrument.

"Antoine," she said after a while, "do you know I love this much more than going to the ball?"

"That is because you do not fancy any one of the party. What do you expect, Annette? Our young men here have wealth, some of them are of good birth, some even of rank. There are De Bardeau, the De Moutbrun. Why do you dislike Baptiste so much?"

"Chut!" said Annette, looking annoyed, "never mention him to me."

"Not mention him to you when he made you queen at the last 'King's ball'?"

"I care not to play the queen to Baptiste in the role of king," she said haughtily.

Antoine's question, "What do you expect?" had aroused a vague interest in her. What was it? Not wealth alone. Fine looks? No, that of course, but more. Was she too aspiring,

looked too high, and out of all reason, for her?
No, it was not that either. Her young nature
was putting forth antennæ, reaching out for her
own. Would she ever find *her own?* The dull
flush came into her face as a half perception presented itself.

She laid down the instrument and turned aside
as if unwilling to acknowledge this thought.

Antoine exclaimed, "Oh, not yet."

"Yes," she replied, "it is gone."

Antoine well understood her moods. He knew
that all melody had left her soul. And as he
had often said, "You cannot play unless it is
first in the soul," he did not urge her, but continued alone to run over the remaining passages.

Annette crossed the attic to where stood a
trunk obsolete in style, now used as a receptacle
for old letters. These were mostly in French,
but some were in German, left by an old, eccen-
tric professor from a German university, who in
the course of his wanderings had reached the
settlement in the wilderness. He had taught
Antoine what knowledge he possessed of the instrument when Antoine was a small lad. Antoine's present skill had developed with his years,
natural gifts supplying the lack of instruction.

"Why does papa keep all of this rubbish? It should be destroyed. Only the rats gain from it," said Annette.

"Perhaps future generations may, if ever there should be such a mad rage for old documents in this country as once there was in Florence."

"When was that?"

"In the fifteenth century, when men would invest a fortune in an old manuscript."

"That is like what Ma'm'selle told us of Holland and the speculations in tulip bulbs. How amusing it must have been to hear those grave old professors discussing the merits of this or that particular bulb, and of the rise or fall in the market."

"What, do you think that there will ever be as much mistaken zeal in this land, Antoine?"

"Humuli souli," replied Antoine abruptly. He caught an expression occasionally from his political elders. Stray sentences here and there, at long intervals, may have been the pebbles dropped into the current of passing events that caused the ever increasing ripple of widely diffused waves of influence.

Annette did not understand him, nor did he himself understand the full import of his remark.

Then the talk drifted away to local matters until Rose interrupted them by pounding on the lowest step and calling out: "Hey, up dere! Ma'm'selle Marie is at de gate, an' she say it am time for de lessons. Do you hyah?"

Annette arose quickly, brushing against a hunter's outfit of deerskin, the cap, with its fox-brush attached, flapping in her face as she passed to the door.

"Adieu," called Antoine gayly, as she hastened to meet Marie.

She gave him a parting smile and disappeared.

"Rose," said Annette, "papa has gone to the other river, and may not be back to lunch."

"Very well, Ma'm'selle. I'll sabe him a bit of something. T'ink the Monsieur right well dese days, honey?" Rose had a soft spot in her heart for old master, as she called him to herself, but she never forgot the Monsieur before others. "She had to keep up wid dose French niggers shure, even if dey did trip around wid deir noses in the air, and their manners so mightily fine. Dey dassent laud it over black Rose, sho now."

"Oh, yes, Rose," answered Annette decidedly. "Appetite lags in the spring."

"'Tisn't dat, 'zactly," began Rose.

Annette didn't wait to encourage further observations on the part of Rose.

She found Marie seated upon the wooden settee that was placed near the door in the wide hall. Later in the season it would be moved out on the gallery.

CHAPTER V.

BAPTISTE.

"ANNETTE," said the young girl, jumping up to meet her friend, "we are late. Ma'm'selle will despair and say that we have no interest and are giddy and frivolous like other girls.

"Let us, then, not stand here longer," said Annette, with roguish eyes, as she put on her white sun-bonnet, and they started down the walk to the gate.

Annette and Marie, "inseparable," said their friends. Marie, petite, tender, every movement instinct with grace; Annette, calm usually to stateliness, but, if the mood were upon her, a mocking gayety or a hidden restlessness would come to the surface and beyond her control.

Later in the season the village street would be brilliant with the flowers that bloomed in the gardens, which were arranged so tastefully. Marie had a knot of sweet violets at her belt, which exhaled their aroma as she moved.

Annette spoke of them in a complimentary way.

"Ah, yes," said Marie carelessly, "Baptiste handed the bunch to me on my way to you."

"Marie, I wish you to have nothing to do with him."

"Why not, *ma belle cousine?*" (opening her eyes.) *Cousine* was a term of endearment in this case, the girls being warmly attached. "He is handsome and bows with such an air, no matter if he is in hunting suit—that old deerskin, you remember—and when he happens to meet with a crowd of us, his manners are perfect. He cannot be surprised out of them."

"All of our young men can do that, but—he fawns upon the rich—Marie, it is sickening," said Annette, disdainfully.

"Ah," replied Marie, naively, "I have not wealth, so have not been made to suffer."

Annette laughed.

"He keeps the books well for General Edgar; he is good in business, is he not, Annette?"

"That goes without saying," said her friend. "But that cannot make me like him, Marie. Good business habits he may have acquired, but it is he himself that is distasteful to me."

"He is well connected," ventured Marie.

"There it is.   I am not speaking of the merits of his family."

"Oh, Annette, do not bite so this morning." "What a lovely pink! See, Annette," she called out in glee.   They were passing a store where the merchant was holding up a muslin for the inspection of a customer.

The French girls and women, even in early times, were quick to follow the fashions of New Orleans, or even of France.   The going and coming of friends was the medium of information.   Elegant dresses were not entirely unknown. In after days, when the State capital was removed to Vandalia, and the 'Kaskia ladies attended the balls and parties of the season, they were long remembered for their gay and rich dress.

"Marie, did I hear you say that we were late?" teased Annette.

"Oui, oui," said Marie, looking regretfully after the pink muslin.   "Come, I will hurry, and do you, Annette."

By this time they were in the midst of the general traffic of the place.   Different nationalities were represented, mostly French, numbers

of English, also Americans, and some Irish.
Indians came for supplies all the way from the
far distant Rocky Mountains.

They passed a group of the savages. The
warriors wore their coarse black hair in braids
on either side of their faces; feathers stood out
from their heads in a hideous, grotesque style.
Beads were suspended from their ears. Black
and red paint ornamented the faces of one or
two. The squaws were equally repulsive. Dirty
red blankets trailed from their shoulders; their
legs were bare, with worn moccasins on their feet.
A pappoose was strapped on the back of the last
one.

"Our Kaskaskia Indians are much beyond these
in comparison," said Marie, with a grimace.

"The Jesuits civilized them ages ago and
taught them the arts of the white man," replied
Annette.

"You have read what Father Charlevoix said
in 1721, almost a hundred years ago? He spoke
of the flourishing Jesuit mission he found at
'Kaskia, and of the ease in which the Indians
lived. He wrote of their industry, and that they
tilled the ground, had swine and black cattle,
even raised poultry. The women spun the wool

of the buffalo into threads as fine as those made from English sheep, and even dyed the stuff woven."

"How have they fallen away, then?" asked Marie.

"That was in their palmy days. First an Indian village, then a Jesuit mission, afterwards a trading center, and now to what does 'Kaskia aspire?"

"To be State capital, of course," responded Marie, repeating the words parrot-like.

They stopped to let a charette cross the road —a small wooden affair, with the ponies harnessed one in front of the other. It would hold about three times as much as a wheelbarrow of to-day. Many shabby uniforms were abroad, men saving expense in buying old stores cheap, though actual service had been seen by a large number.

Emigrants poured in at this season of the year, trying to secure grants to "heads of families," and government bounties had claimants. The country was now rescued from Indian depredations, and settlers were founding homes in the surrounding section, and were scattering as to locality.

The early colonists clung together, partly through a sense of common danger, but the French instinct was to cluster for social pleasure, rather than live in the isolation of a farm-house. The old French grants of so many "arpents" were laid off in narrow strips, all running toward the river, or from bluffs to river, but the people lived in villages.

As they passed the land office, Annette, who had been in a brown study upon these questions, looked around and said:

"Now this is what I spoke of yesterday, Marie. I like not the queer mixture of home-seekers."

"Why not?" said Marie. "You would not grudge them homes when land is to be had almost for the asking?"

"No, no. I do not mean," she said quickly at this view of her feeling—"not that. Let them have all they want—all, all. It is something else."

Probably she could not have defined the subtle feeling to herself, but it was the externals that grated upon her. Elements as yet were not assorted or harmonious with existing conditions.

They soon arrived at their destination—a house built with the favorite outside chimney, and having two tiny rectangular windows just under the gable. The extensive grounds fell toward the river in the rear. Bright yellow dandelions dotted the grassy slope.

"Gainckon and the colt are in for the day," said Marie. "See, she is training the colt, is it not so, Annette?"

They paused to admire the free, really splendid movement of the mother, the young animal scampering at her heels. There seemed to be something of a definite plan on the part of the mother, for she tried again and again the same round.

"The promise of a 'Sleepy Davie,'" said Annette.

"Bravo!"

Miss Somers, the English lady, appeared at the entrance. They opened the latch of the gate and hastened to meet her.

"Pardon, Ma'm'selle," said Marie. "The air this spring is beguiling, and we lag sadly on the way."

CHAPTER VI.

THEY were ushered into a room occupied by the sweet controlling spirit of that household, a woman whose surroundings at once appealed to one's inward sense of approval.

The hangings attached to the high "four-poster" were of white dimity edged with lace. The coverlid and pillows were spotless. A fresh gown, hands neatly attended to, betokened watchful and loving care on the part of some one.

A paralyzed, helpless left arm and hand lay at her side, but the eager, bright eyes showed that the mind was active and alert, and that outside interests were not forgotten or viewed with indifference by Madame Chartran, shut in these twelve years past.

"Bon jour, Madame."

"Bon jour," smiling cordially.

"How is the health of Madame?" asked Annette, turning to Miss Somers, who stood near the bed.

"This is one of her comfortable days," answered Miss Somers in a prim way. She had been a governess so long that her manners had become set in consequence of taking the character of a model of behavior, which goes with the position as a necessary qualification. Naturally she was a warm-hearted woman, and not a machine.

"Now," said Miss Somers, "first our drawing lesson, then the reading. I have a change for you to-day in the books."

Materials were placed on the table, and the latter was drawn into a good light. Miss Somers placed a brown earthen pitcher, containing a spray of wild flowers, in position for a study.

"Ma'm'selle, are we not soon to sketch the church? Did you not advise us to make a drawing before the church was torn down?"

"There is time," said Madame Chartran. "The church may last for years. Little interest; slow progress."

"Some say if a new church is built, then nothing less than a convent will follow, and they shake their heads at that, and say, 'Too much cost.'"

"Doubtless that will follow—after many years," said Miss Somers with a prim little smile.

She had spent but a year with her sister, but she fully realized the difference in methods between the bustling manufacturing city of her birth and the quiet, sleepy village of these old-time French. There was money enough, but not desire sufficient, as yet, for the innovation.

"Ah, but," said Madame, "a more active spirit is approaching. There is talk of making a State of the Territory, and that will bring more people here. Colonel Menard and Shadrach Bond, Dr. Fisher, young Kane and Judge Thomas are endeavoring to bring this about."

"Not all will come to us, for new settlements will spring up and will draw away from our village," said Marie,

"Come now, it is time for the reading," said Miss Somers, glancing up at the tall clock in the corner.

The girls were curious to know what she had in store for them.

"Last week a box from England came by way of Vincennes, and some of my books that I had left at home came to light in the unpacking. Among them was 'Corinne' in the original. Marie, that will please you."

"It will be a change from the dry history,"
said Marie.

"Madame De Stael is both witty and wise. I
wish you to hear her views on Italy and her
descriptions of art. We will read some extracts."

"I heard papa and the German professor, a
long time ago, commenting on Madame de Stael.
They said she had all the powers to lead in conversation," said Annette.

"So she had, so she had. You have heard that
the Emperor was extremely fond of her."

"No," said Marie innocently, "was he?"

Madame Chartran and her sister laughed.

"No, child," said Madame, "he disliked and
feared her, and finally sent her away from
France."

"Poor lady! that must have been hard. To
have to leave Paris, alas!"

"So, Marie, Paris was the end of all things to
be desired in this world?"

"Then perhaps we would not have had
'Corinne,' but she liked to be known as a literary
celebrity."

"Sister," turning her eyes upon Miss Somers,
"I have heard some talk of her marriage to M.
de Rocca. Some believed it, others disputed it."

"Mamma wrote home in one of her letters of the gossip going around in regard to Madame de Stael, but she stated not as to the truth of it."

"Let us commence the reading," said Miss Somers. "We chatter more than we read."

The next hour was spent in a delightful manner. Enchanting descriptions of scenery, palaces of art, the customs of a political people, eloquent remarks upon Italian literature. The glowing and fervid language fell upon deeply interested listeners.

After the reading was ended, the two girls bade adieu to Madame and her sister, and took their departure.

"Madame met her husband in Canada, did she not?" asked Marie.

"Yes," said Annette.

CHAPTER VII.

THE PROSPECT.

MONSIEUR BEAUVAIS rode out of the village at a slow canter. He was never in a hurry, for he lacked the zeal that arises from a deep-seated interest in the affairs of life. That he prospered was more on account of his being a part of the times than any effort put forth by him.

His sturdy pony carried him along a trail that led past the lodges from which he had, at start-ing, noticed the rising smoke. A lazy indolence was about the camp. Some of the squaws were planting corn in small garden patches.

The wheat was green in the "common fields." Large numbers of cattle were grazing on the rich prairie grass of the commons. The beauty of the early spring was over the land and be-tween the two rivers. The mild climate and ex-ceedingly rich soil produced an abundant yield. Cotton, corn, hemp, grains and European fruits were among the products.

Monsieur Beauvais' plantation bordered the
Mississippi, and was four miles from the village.
As he proceeded on his way his thoughts turned
away from the past, and dwelt upon his children.

"Antoine will have the land," he mused, "and
there is no better around here. I have provided
for that." A troubled look came into his face as
an ill-defined foreboding passed over him. "He
is a fine fellow, and apparently does not care to
accumulate. I have not set him the example.
But increase may not come as easily to the next
generation as to this one, and he may need to
exert himself more to hold what belongs to his
share. What was it that Seneca said? 'He
who careth not for riches is already rich,' or
words to that effect. Bah! that would do for him
to say, *prædives* as he was. He could not
know by experience. It is easy for one to
prescribe another's duty."

An amused smile played about his lips as he
remembered a remark made by a neighbor's
daughter:

"Ah, yes," said Loisee, "my married sister
comes home and says, 'Ta, ta. You would not
leave mamma in her failing health. Why, it is
your duty to stay with her.' 'And, pray, why

was it not your duty to stay?' I answer grimly."

"Now that reminds me of Annette. Provision should be made for her settlement.   In France," he thought, "if her angel mother"— ,

And he sighed.   "What ought one to do? Women always know how to manage such things. Old Rose said but the other day:

"'Monsieur, time Ma'm'selle looking 'round.'

"'Looking around?'

"'Yes, lookin' 'round, I tell you. She too highty, Monsieur. I heah de young men say dat.'

"'There is time yet, Rose.' But Rose shook her head."

Monsieur's thoughts were in an unwonted channel, and in such a deep study was he that he did not hear the sound of hoofs just behind him.

A clear voice called out: "Bon jour, Monsieur."

"Bon jour, Monsieur Bond."

"A beautiful morning for a ride, sir."

"Oui," responded Monsieur Beauvais, "and how is your health and that of your family?"

"Quite well, I am pleased to say," answered Shadrach Bond. A man very popular, a pioneer of great and noble talents. The following year he was elected Governor of the new State. He possessed a striking face, clear-cut features, a fine forehead, a long, aquiline nose, a mouth whose lips could curl in haughty disdain, if the occasion required.

"You are well, and your daughter, the handsome Ma'm'selle?"

"I thank you, yes."

"The young Annette is fast being transformed into an attractive woman, Monsieur."

"Yes," said Monsieur Beauvais, frowning slightly.

"I hear that Antoine desires to go down with the next cargo. Is that true, Monsieur?"

"He wishes it, but I have not yet made my decision. Antoine is a good son, but the journey takes much time. Town life is not the thing for a country-grown lad like Antoine, Monsieur Bond, but he begs hard for it."

"Ah, well," said Shadrach Bond, "youth longs for change, and a man must see something of the world, if the world is a wilderness. More will be expected of the youth of the next generation. These are changing times." And his eyes brightened as he continued: "It will not

be long before we rejoice in the honor of a
State, and what a glorious State will our Illinois
Territory become! Think of her resources, of
the homes that are to be, as these prairies are
filled by those needing and seeking homes.
The abundance that the land brings forth will
feed thousands. She will be an illustration of
the line that 'Westward the star of empire takes
its march.'" His countenance beamed with enthusiasm, and he unconsciously drew himself up
as this vision appeared before his mind.

"Oh," said Monsieur Beauvais, pettishly, "are
we not well enough as we are? The villagers
lead such peaceful, happy lives. We have sufficient for our wants, and these strangers coming
in will only annoy and confuse us. I for one
think that it is too soon to advance such ideas.
There is time for that in the future."

Shadrach Bond looked at him curiously, but
he remembered Monsieur's habits of life; that
he could not bear any disturbance in the usual
routine—the breakfast, assorting his papers and
simple accounts, a little exercise in the garden,
a book, an early dinner, a nap, a chat with a
neighbor, a walk by the river in season.

"A man of another age and country, not of

ours," thought Shadrach Bond. "The time is approaching, whether we seek it or not," he said gravely. "I, on the 'other hand, am most anxious to bring about this very thing. I am on my way to Dr. Fisher to consult with him on this question, and hear his counsel. His ideas are excellent, and he is a power to be sought, and held on the right side. Here is the turning-off place to Dr. Fisher's settlement. Good-day, Monsieur." And he touched his spirited horse and galloped away.

"Monsieur Bond has great feelings," mused M. Beauvais, "but why can he not be content to let matters remain as they are? I am quite in a flutter at the thought of such change. I cannot compose myself." And he endeavored to turn his thoughts to other matters.

When he was disturbed, certain sensations would pass over him, and a queer waving in the head would trouble him for a short time. But as he neared his plantation he became more cheerful. The place was well kept. The fields were in corn. Large herds of cattle were grazing. In the winter they would be driven into the canebrakes to fatten.

"Henri must get out the rest of the hides and

have them ready for the boats," he thought.
"Henri, Henri," he called as he rode up to the
door of a log cabin.

Henri was seated on a log cutting potatoes for
early planting. The old Frenchman, whose
smooth face was as brown as an Indian's, arose
and came forward.

"Are you getting along with the work, Henri?"

"Oui, oui, Monsieur."

"The corn is in the ground early.   The garden
does well.   And how is Therese?"

"In good health, I thank you."

"Take the pony out to a stable while I stay,"
said Monsieur Beauvais to a round-faced lad that
came from the stable.

This was young Henri, who was all devotion
to Antoine, and who was his faithful shadow
when Antoine came over for a hunt or a tramp.
In the fall they had great sport on the island,
hunting wild ducks.   Henri was disappointed
when he saw that Monsieur was alone.

Monsieur Beauvais went with Henri to inspect
a young orchard at the back of the cabin.
Henri explained the process of planting, which
he thought was just right because that was the
way the trees were set out when he lived with

ELIAS KENT KANE,
UNITED STATES SENATOR.

SHADRACH BOND,
THE FIRST GOVERNOR OF ILLINOIS.

Colonel Menard. However, Monsieur Beauvais was not hard to please.

"It is all very well done, very well, indeed."

After he had given his orders for a shipment, M. Beauvais returned to the cabin for a cup of black coffee before starting on the return ride. The April sun was pleasant; the bees were humming. He leaned back against the house with an air of contentment. As to whether the Illinois country was a State or Territory, just then, was matter of little moment to him.

Henri, the lad with the good-natured face, asked him respectfully: "Will Antoine be over soon, Monsieur?"

"Antoine has wild thoughts in his head. He wants to go down on the *bateau* this voyage."

Young Henri looked disappointed. "May I go too, Monsieur?" he said, lifting large, expectant eyes to the other.

Monsieur shrugged his shoulders. "For why? You are all needed on the plantation. It cannot be," he answered indifferently.

He did not see the look of resolution that passed over the face of the boy, who inwardly resolved that if Antoine went down the river, he, Henri, would be with him.

Presently Monsieur called for his pony, and started for old 'Kaskia at the same gentle pace with which he had left in the morning.

"What was the boy thinking of to ask me such a question? What with men carried away by politics, and the youth wanting to leave, the country is going to ruin. It wasn't so when I was young. I cannot reason with Antoine and persuade him out of this foolish notion. Henri too!" And Monsieur Beauvais laughed at the thought.

CHAPTER VIII.

THE GALLERY.

THAT evening Annette and Papa Beauvais were sitting on the long gallery that extended around the entire front of the house. The air was mild, the sun fairly down, but with a yellow haze to cover its retreat. Annette was at one end, where a climbing rose covered a framework built for its support. She was idly picking the green leaves to pieces. Papa Beauvais had given the details of his ride, and had expressed his satisfaction with Henri and his management of the plantation. Antoine had gone to the river. Annette's attention was aroused by some one entering the gate. The horseman of the previous day came smiling up the walk.

Annette's listlessness was gone. Greetings were exchanged, and a lively conversation ensued.

"You still wear your scalp, Monsieur," said Annette gayly.

"Oui, Ma'm'selle," said Monsieur St. Gemme,
laying his hand on his dark, wavy hair.

"How far did you ride?" asked Papa Beauvais.

" A great distance, Monsieur, as far as the Sac
and Fox country."

"Annette, you dislike the new-comers. Listen
to this story." And Monsieur laughed.

"Go on," said Annette.

"The Sac village is on Rock River, and the
Fox village on the Mississippi, nearly opposite
the island. Their Good Spirit was as white as
the driven snow. Its voice was as the sweetest
music. Its wings were compared to the swan,
but larger in size. Its home was among the
rocks, in a cavern that no one dared to approach.
On no account would any Indian trespass on
ground that was sacred to its habitation. Hence
the cavern was never disturbed. At rare intervals would this wonderful spirit make its appearance. It was sent by the Great Spirit to guide
the Sac and Fox Indians in the management of
their affairs. The delight of this spirit was in
goodness. But the advent of the Americans so
grieved it that, flying off, it returned to them
again never more."

"The idea is an old one. We wish to fly from

sorrow or what pains and grieves us," said Papa Beauvais.

"Oui." The younger man assented to the remark with a sigh, and unconsciously his glance sought that of Annette and held her for a moment. Monsieur St. Gemme's eyes could grow tender with feeling. Then, as if to banish what had been the fleeting thought, he said, lightly:

"Nevertheless these Americans are infusing new life and spirit into the territory. Commerce is widening. Our sleepy French ways are being left behind. Our Indian trade is extending and making us rich. St. Louis is having her share. She is a formidable rival to us, Monsieur."

"We have much the start," he said condescendingly. "Where is Antoine?"

"Ah, there he is! The youth is bent on a voyage. Are you to go?"

"It may be. The plans are not all made."

"What does Josephine say to these frequent absences on your part?" inquired Annette.

"She says that it is equal to being a widow, and that she is even now looking out for my successor," he answered jestingly.

Monsieur St. Gemme had been a constant
visitor to the house for a number of years. Monsieur Beauvais had taken a fancy to the young
man's company.

St. Gemme possessed a great deal of tact.
His nature was one on which a weaker nature
would rely. For one of his age he was a good
judge of other men. Important business was
intrusted to his care, and he was usually successful in its transaction.

He had married into a wealthy family. It
was one of those matches arranged according to
the French custom, in which the parents made
the choice and all arrangements in the contract.
Monsieur St. Gemme had been a kind husband,
and Josephine apparently was a contented wife,
and doubtless a happy one. Her two children
filled her life so completely that all other interests were but secondary matters.

"I wish you to influence Antoine to remain at
home. I like not the idea of his going."

"I will try," said Monsieur St. Gemme.

Antoine and Baptiste came up the street just
then. They joined the group on the gallery,
and the conversation became general.

Ere long Baptiste seated himself on the bench
by the side of Annette.

She felt annoyed, but was too polite to show it.

"Annette," said he, looking at her with bold admiration. (A dull flush came into her face, and her eyes flashed). "Do you remember the rose that you gave me from this bush last year? I have it yet."

"Have you?" She was very indifferent to his remarks. She had not in fact given the rose to him. He had picked it up and asked her permission to retain it.

"That is one year ago," he repeated softly. "You have changed much in that time."

"Ah, you mistake, I am just the same," she said, accenting slightly the last of her sentence.

"I mean that you are growing handsome;" he said quickly.

"Baptiste, do not say such things to me. I like them not."

"A young ma'm'selle, and she is not to hear of her beauty. I have had other experience than that. Annette, Annette," he said under cover of the conversation of the others, "why am I so disagreeable to you? Your manner would imply that I have no right to live, that I incumber the ground."

"If you judge that to be my thought, why do you persist in saying those things that are not welcome to me?"

"Why does the flower turn toward the sun? Why does the bee seek the flower? Are we responsible for the interest that leads us to that which attracts beyond all else?" he said fervently.

"Baptiste, can you not, will you not understand?" she began.

But suddenly he began to talk of other subjects. The next ball—would she be there? He did not know whether they would make another "King's ball" of it or not. The matter was not decided.

"Is it not too bad that Antoine will miss this one?"

"Papa has not yet given his consent to Antoine, and he seems very reluctant to do so," said Annette.

Monsieur St. Gemme arose to go. Annette made this an excuse for leaving Baptiste.

"Can you make a straight line yet? How do the lessons progress under the Ma'm'selle?"

"Ma'm'selle is very kind."

"Do not spoil your lovely eyes over that sort of study, Annette. It is not worth it."

"We do not apply ourselves to that extent," laughed Annette. "I fear that it is only pastime with us, and that we have not the true leaning toward art."

"I bid you good night, Ma'm'selle."

"Good night, Monsieur."

After taking a courteous leave of the others, he started down the street with a quick, springing step.

CHAPTER IX.

"A mixture of books, education and backwoods activity produces the greatest of men."—Reynolds' Pioneer History of Illinois.

SHADRACH BOND, after leaving Monsieur Beauvais, kept his horse to a brisk canter. He was a man of superior judgment, and much practical knowledge of the motives that are the springs of human action. This insight into character was of service to him in various positions of trust which he filled when working for the interests of the people. An act of Congress giving the people the right of pre-emption as settlers was due to his exertions, and he deserved the gratitude of all that section of country in consequence. This act was passed in 1813. The way was thus opened to emigration, and the public lands placed upon the market. Bond had been elected the first Delegate from the Territory to Congress. It was thought that he would be chosen the first Governor, as the confidence and affection of the people were his.

In person he was tall; his bearing was dignified
and commanding. The ride on this bright morning was exhilarating to one whose activity of
mind and body needed some outlet to energy.

In a short time he arrived at Dr. Fisher's settlement, which was near the bluffs about six
miles above Kaskaskia.

Dr. Fisher was Speaker of the House in the
Territorial government.

"Ah, Bond," called the Doctor on his approach.
"A fine day."

"Good morning, Doctor."

"What news have you, Bond?"

"I saw the persons to whom you referred.
Everything is doing well in that quarter. Nathaniel Pope is making his arrangements to push
the matter before the House next session."

"He certainly has our interests enough at
heart to do his best."

"The question is this, will Congress pass the
act to call the convention?"

"That is coming. I have not a doubt of it,"
said Fisher earnestly. "And within a year, I
prophesy. What is the prevalent idea with respect to the Constitution?"

"I do not know. All want a Constitution,"

said Shadrach Bond. "I met a conservative Frenchman on the way—Monsieur Beauvais. He would not favor any change from existing conditions. But you and I realize that a future is to be provided for, the emergencies of which must be met."

"Yes, and a grand future. See how this country is filling up the past three years.

An organization to secure equal rights to individuals and to protect their privileges is required. It is high time we were wheeling into line with the rest of the States. The dignity of our growing population demands recognition."

Dr. Fisher was leaning against a corner of the block house.

"Times have changed since that was built," said Bond significantly.

"Yes," said Dr. Fisher, "that represents a rapidly vanishing past."

Both men gazed upon the building in silent thought. It was a story and a half high, built of great, strong logs. Portholes were in the lower story for shooting through. The heavy puncheon door stood wide open. Formerly it had been provided with thick bars to keep out the Indians. The second story projected over the lower about four feet. This also had holes in the floor projecting beyond the lower part, through which the pioneer could shoot down upon Indians trying to force an entrance. The remains of a stockade extended a short distance beyond the corners.

"Yes, these were the bulwarks of the frontier, and but for them none would be left to discuss the advantages to be gained in the transition from Territory to State."

There was a curious mixture on the Doctor's premises. The dwellings were comfortable, but there were other structures that had been used as a small-pox hospital in 1801. Two or three cases had been brought from "Pain Court" (St. Louis). The village had been put in quarantine, but nearly the whole population had passed through the scourge under Dr. Fisher's care.

"The Territorial legislature will meet on the fifth of December," said Bond.

"In the case of the Governors and Lieutenant Governors men desire that these should be elected by the people."

"They also favor a single term of office for Governor, and that he shall not be eligible to re-election. The *viva voce* method of voting is the popular idea."

"The judges of the inferior courts are to hold office during good behavior," said Fisher.

"I know of some who will go out of office then," replied Bond, laughing as he took his departure.

CHAPTER X.

OLD ROSE and Annette were in a great flutter. Antoine was to leave on the following day. The hesitation and objection of Monsieur Beauvais had been talked down, discussed, brought up again, reviewed, and in the end overcome.

Francis Menard promised to take Antoine in his charge. Every one knew what Menard was a natural *voyageur*, brave, daring almost to recklessness. A storm that would frighten other men, and cause them to run in to shore, he would utilize to carry him that much farther on his way and save thereby much wearisome labor. His men had every confidence in his skill, and would follow him to any length, and he invariably brought them safely out of an adventure.

To Antoine, simple villager as he was, who had never been more than a score of miles away from home, the prospect was exciting, and in anticipation of the new and unusual scenes awaiting him his spirits were at the highest pitch.

. "Annette, do not forget the music and the 'vi'lin,' as old Rose has it."

"Antoine, you will not have the need of these while gone."

"Why not? At full moon, as we glide over the sparkling water, what would my soul desire more than the companionship of music? The red man will start from his dreams in the wigwam on the shore, and think that the Great Spirit is calling him, as a seeming strain from the mighty hunting ground is heard across the water."

"The instrument will be in your way. You will forget it in the town. What shall I do, *both* gone?"

"Ah, that is even so. I will not deprive you of the music. You would miss that more than Antoine."

"Ah, no, it is you that I shall sadly miss." And her beautiful eyes filled with tears at the thought of the long separation.

Hardly a day had passed that they had not seen one another. Their earliest recollections were of wandering hand in hand over the "commons," searching for wild flowers—two motherless children.

FIRST BRICK HOUSE WEST OF THE ALLEGHENY MOUNTAINS.

"Do you remember this picture, Antoine?" said Annette. It was a miniature of Marie and herself.

Antoine gazed upon it fondly. "I would not take anything for it."

"Frazine always told me I must have one taken if the chance ever occurred to me."

"Do you remember when the Indians scared us so?" resumed Annette.

"I do, Annette," he replied, laughing. "Your two eyes were like saucers, and your teeth chattered until I thought they would drop out."

"You were the same," she retorted.

"I can see Risden now, stretched out full length before the great chimney. Frazine was telling you a story."

Risden and Frazine were two young darkies, brother and sister, that Monsieur had secured by indenture. Frazine was nurse to Annette after the death of the French Babette.

"Yes, and a wild whoop made us jump to our feet, and I began to cry," said Annette.

"The biggest one pounded on the door and asked for some coals."

"How angry he was when the door was not opened. They all yelled and danced about the house."

"They were from the Rockies."

"Papa was away with Joseph Buyatte; he had the fever."

"And the neighbors were gone to the ball."

"Frazine told me to run and hide, or the Indians would get me sure and carry me off."

"You ran and hid under the bed up-stairs. What then, Annette?"

"I was nearly dead with fright. I said ten Ave Marias as fast as I could."

"They knew we were afraid of them, so they kept up the din a great while," said Antoine. "Every time the fire threw a black shadow on the wall, I thought it was a big Indian ready to clutch me. What hard times children have. They suffer so with fright, and grown people do not realize their terror."

"Do you remember Frazine's favorite way of getting us quiet, so that she could go off and have a good frolic with the slaves? She would put us to bed and tell us to cover our heads, and that if we stirred Rawbones and Bloody Head would get us. And there we would be, paralyzed in our terror, and keep as still as mice."

"Yes, and to keep us from telling papa, she would say you must never speak the name, or

this terrible creature would come for us that
night."

Antoine drew down his face and looked so
lugubrious that Annette laughed heartily.

"Frazine and Risden did fight like savages.
Papa grew tired of their fussing, and so, one
day, he brought home switches of the water-
willows, and gave one to Risden and one to
Frazine, and kept one in his own hand. 'Now,'
he said, 'this must end. You, Risden, are to
whip Frazine; you, Frazine, are to whip Risden.
Get at it as fast as you can, or I will whip the
one that lags.' I shall never forget that day.
I thought papa was a hard, hard man. When-
ever Risden would strike Frazine with the whip
I would scream as lustily as I could. I loved
Frazine, and I could not bear to have her hurt.
I screamed aloud and ran to her, and threw my
arms about her, so that papa had to desist.
But that was the last of their quarrels for a few
weeks. Papa sent Frazine away afterwards.
Frazine told me that God would give me anything that I would pray for. I used to go off by
myself and pray that God would send me my
mamma."

"That was something she heard in Virginia,

before she was brought to 'Kaskia," said Antoine.

A wistful look was in Annette's eyes as she spoke of the "pretty mamma" her baby lips had called after Frazine—a sense of something missed — an experience that belonged to the life of other girls, but which she herself would never know.

"Come, Annette, you must not be sad on this, my last day."

"No, I must be gay," she said in a brighter tone, but she felt a deep foreboding at this break in their family circle.

They went out to the kitchen, where black Rose was in the act of hanging a pot on the end of the crane. The blazing coals brought out the drops of perspiration on her forehead.

"Who dere?" she said, turning to look at the brother and sister as they entered. "You gwine to leave old Rose, for sure. Not much use frizzing over the cookin' when you gone, Antoine. Monsieur don't eat nuffin, and Ma'm'selle picks like de little robin."

"What shall I bring Rose? A new apron, or a pair of satin slippers?"

"Go along wid your satin slippers. Dem old moccasins good enough for Rose any day," holding up one foot, with a big hole in the moccasin.

"Soon be de hot weather. Don' need nothin' but nature's dressin' on me foot den," she said, grinning and chuckling, her eyes snapping and blinking as she shook her head. "Antoine, you be a good chile, and don't get no bad ways off der. You heah?"

"Not I, Rose," said Antoine, and made her a mock bow, as he left.

"Dat boy 'pears like he a perfect gem'man. Always so perlite. But I dun know what Monsieur tinking of to let him go away by hisself. 'Pears to Rose dat it's not a good ting, somehow. But here comes dat Monsieur St. Gemme and dat impudent Jule, both on dem 'p'int ponies.' "*

"Ah, Rose, good morning; brewing for dinner?" said Monsieur St. Gemme, as a savory odor greeted him from the kitchen.

"Making bouillon, Monsieur. Hab some?"

"Not just now, Rose. Is Monsieur Beauvais at home?"

As Monsieur St. Gemme disappeared around the corner Jule commenced to worry Rose with his French.

* Ponies caught in the point from the herd of wild horses that had escaped from the French, and had there multiplied. These ponies had great endurance.

"Yi, yi," muttered Rose, turning her back to the smiling Jule.

"Say, Rose, get bouillon for Jule?"

"You, Jule! I's nothing for the likes of you," she said, sniffing contemptuously, and, completely ignoring him, she set about her work.

"Ah," said Monsieur, coming out from his garden, and greeting his guest, "I shall have early peas in two weeks."

"I congratulate you.   Has Antoine his preparation completed?   Francis Menard tells me that the bateau will start at the break of day."

"How long the absence this time?"

"It will require at least six months for the voyage."

"So long? Well, I must make up my mind not to fret.   Come in, come in."   And, suiting the action to the word, he led the way.

Monsieur Beauvais offered the visitor some light wine that was in the decanter on the sideboard.   As he reached out his arm to hand the glass to Monsieur St. Gemme, all at once his head swam, a great dizziness overcame him, and he appeared about to fall.

The younger man sprang to his side instantly, in great surprise, as he had never seen Monsieur Beauvais so afflicted.

"What can I do?" he began to say, but consciousness returned to Monsieur Beauvais, and with it a slow realization of the attack. A look of consternation crossed the old man's face. He drew back with a feeble motion, and said indistinctly:

"It is nothing; pray do not notice. Stooping in the garden, and the sun was overpowering Some wine, please."

Monsieur St. Gemme poured out a glass of vin de Bordeaux for him, and in a few minutes Monsieur Beauvais seemed to be himself again.

"I beg of you, Monsieur St. Gemme, say nothing of this to my children. Antoine must not be disappointed at this late hour, and Annette must not be worried," he added in a lower voice.

After a discussion of Monsieur Beauvais' plan for Antoine in regard to the estate, Monsieur St. Gemme, politely expressing his wish for his friend's restored health, departed.

Monsieur Beauvais went to his own apartment, and, going to his desk in one corner, he opened a small drawer, taking therefrom a tiny case, inclosing a miniature painted on ivory. It was the face of his never forgotten and dearly beloved young wife.

"The time is drawing nearer. No more parting or sorrow over there."

After gazing long at the beautiful countenance, he reverently placed the case in the drawer and locked it.

He lay down upon his couch, and, falling asleep, he did not appear for dinner—a most unheard-of thing.

CHAPTER XI.

THE next morning at daylight a group of men might have been seen wending their way from the church toward the river. They had been to early mass. Francis Menard's invariable custom was to have mass said at the beginning and end of each voyage.

Rose had arisen in the small hours of the night in order that Antoine should have his wants supplied. Antoine would meet the others at the bateau. He hardly swallowed the breakfast that Rose had provided, which consisted of bread in the form of a johnny cake that had been baked on a board placed before the hot coals, a cup of black coffee, and a slice of bacon.

Antoine had bidden farewell to Monsieur Beauvais the night previous, that the morning nap might not be disturbed.

"Good-by, Annette; good-by, Rose." And the

81

youth turned away hastily, that they might not see the tears in his eyes.

Risden was at hand to carry the bag and hunting outfit. A brisk scene awaited Antoine. About fifty flatboatmen were scattered on the shore and in the bateau. Francis Menard was hurrying up the slaves that were carrying in the last load. Two or three merchants were making final arrangements as to the shipment, and also for the goods to be brought on the return trip. Flour, dried beef, skins, pork and great piles of furs taken in the Indian trade were sent to New Orleans and way ports, of which there were but few.

"Ha, Antoine," said Francis Menard, not unkindly, "ready for a rough life, lad?" He looked inquiringly at the youth.

"Quite, Capitaine. At this season not so hard—will it be?"

"Hard enough at all seasons. Wait for the return pull and the *cordelle*. All have to take their turn, you understand?"

"Oui, oui, Capitaine."

"Antoine, be not carried away with the strange sights. Do you have a care and not be deceived as to your companions," said Monsieur St.

Gemme, in an aside. "Do you think always that Annette will constantly have you in mind."

"Oui, Monsieur," answered the youth, with strong feelings. "You will have a care. Papa and Annette—should anything happen, you will be at hand?"

"I promise that right willingly, as if they were my own."

The men were ready by this time. Their voices were lifted in a rhythmic ring to which they plied their oars.

Antoine had clasped Monsieur's hand, and with a spring was on board.

Risden choked in his "Good-by, Antoine. Gloomy times at de home when you is gone."

Antoine waved his hand, and took off his skin cap, and waved it again and again as long as the peaceful village was in sight.

The swift strokes soon brought them into the course of the river and out of sight.

Seven miles below they would enter the Mississippi. 'Kaskia Point lay to their right—the broad expanse of forest land between the forks of the two rivers. They rounded one curve after another. The overhanging cottonwood made dense shadows upon the water, for which they felt through the heavy gray mist. But as they emerged from the mouth of the Okaw (Kaskaskia) River, a rare scene greeted their vision. A roseate hue was in the heavens, and golden rays shot forth toward the distant hills. The mist rose rapidly, and disappeared in a white drift.

The bend is so broad at this point that the river seemed a lake. Some islands a few miles distant showed in graceful outlines the faint green of the water willow.

The great stretches of forest from the shore to the hills in the background, in which the light was dim even at mid-day, confronted them in what was formerly the Spanish country. On their left were some of the most magnificent cliffs to be seen on the Mississippi River. On the top of one of the highest, over 400 feet above them, was an Indian wigwam. It was at the edge of a black oak grove.

"From where yon Indian stands," said Francis Menard, "you can see up and down the river a distance of forty miles."

"See the pawpaw bushes on the side of the bluff and the blackhaws among the tangleweed."

"I have made 'pawpaw harness' many a time," said Menard. "The withes plaited were a substitute for the leather thongs that we now use."

"I do not like the fruit; its taste is too luscious. It sickens me," said Antoine.

An Indian canoe shot out from the point. It was followed by another. The occupants were now busy examining a rude construction for catching fish. This extended from the Illinois shore into the Okaw River.

"There are more lakes in the Spanish country," pointing to the dark forest, "where fish can be had for the catching, and in the fall the air is black with fowl. Rare sport over there."

"We must get the *ccuriers du bois* together this November and bag the game," said Antoine.

"I would like nothing better."

"Look out there, men," said Menard as they were passing the Mary's River, which, swollen at this time, had undermined a large tree, which fell crashing into the water. By quick paddling they escaped its clutches and drew off to a safe distance.

Louis Vallé, a youth near Antoine's age, was in the company. He was going to New Orleans to transact some business for his grandfather, a very wealthy and self-willed old gentleman. Antoine and he were drawn together by the attraction of youth. Most of the men were hardy pioneers, either traders or trappers, or both. They were inured to exposure of every kind.

The bateau had been on its way several hours when some changes were made in the position of the cargo in the hold.

"Capitaine, come here quick. I find a skin that is not tanned." And the trapper smiled broadly.

Menard answered the summons. He looked surprised, then forbidding. "Who is this?" he inquired sternly.

Antoine and Louis, attracted by the bustle, were at his elbow.

"Henri!" exclaimed Antoine as he gazed at the round face of the boy.

Henri was full of confusion and appeared to be somewhat frightened.

"Antoine, Antoine," he cried, "let me stay with you! I could not bear that you should go without me."

"And so you ran away? What will your father do about the crop? Tell me that," Antoine said severely.

"He does not need me. The slaves can do all and more. Antoine, I will do anything, serve

you in any way, if you will but let me stay,"
begged Henri.

"There is no other way now," said Antoine.

"Can you put him at work, Capitaine?" turning toward Menard, and apologizing for the
trouble that Henri was giving him.

"Yes, he shall help the cook; then we may
see."

There were certain regulations to be followed:
Rest at certain intervals; the start each morning at daybreak; camp at nightfall. Then would
the men relax their tired muscles, and, stretched
out at full length on their capotes (blanket-coats
with sleeves) or on bear-skins, recount strange
adventures by the light of the blazing camp-fire.

Henri was happy to be near Antoine. He felt
like a free thing. The monotony of the plantation was far behind him. He listened to the
wild stories of the trappers. A glimpse of
another existence, of which he was on the edge,
crept into his soul.

At the ports the voyageurs were urged to linger
for the festivities that would be pressed upon
them—the instinct, old as history, of the social
nature reaching out after a fellow-creature.

Henri caught the excitement of Antoine as

they approached the crowded levee of *Nouvelle
Orleans.* It was near the dusk of a May evening.
The breeze had already set in from the Gulf.
Five ships were anchored in the river. The
union jack was floating from the mast of one.

"Why are so many people out this evening,
Capitaine? Has anything happened?" asked
Antoine.

"No," laughed Menard, "it is always so as the
bateaux come in. Every one—slaves and all,
that can slip off, come down to hear the news
and take the air."

Loud greetings were called out to Menard as
the bateau drew near. He was a favorite with
the people. He had a frank and sincere manner
that gained him friends everywhere. The merchants with whom he did business were quickly
gathered about him, and the cargo was assigned
by lots and a watch detailed to take charge of
what remained. Then the trappers sought their
old haunts and the exchange of news, and parted
with their money for that which was not news.

Antoine and Louis kept close company with
Menard. The loud French, the Spanish, the
jargon of the foreign tongues, all were confusing
to Antoine. He had thought the mixture famil-

iar to him in one village, but here was bustle and argument and dispute in such rapid succession as to be intensely bewildering to his inexperience. He viewed with admiration the splendor of some Spanish dignitaries. A pirogue containing negro slaves passed up the river. They were singing a musical lay in which the refrain was repeated over and over. Our voyageurs must be lodged for the night, and followed Menard as he pushed through the crowd about the doorways of the cabaret, where men were drinking tafia and others absorbed in gaming.

"Henri, keep near to me," said Antoine. "I don't wish to lose you at this stage. What think you of it, Louis?"

"I intend to see more," said Louis.

"And so will I; but the smell is vile."

CHAPTER XII.

NOUVELLE ORLEANS.

ANTOINE and Louis slept the next morning. Menard and Henri had gone to the levee at an early hour.

"Shall we walk?" asked Antoine.

"By all means," replied Louis.

Their strolling steps led them first to the market. "Fresh fish and fresh vegetables" were being cried, "just from the plantation." They watched Madame, in her smart frock, trying for a cheap bargain. A negress was at hand to carry the basket when filled.

Proceeding along the street, the goods displayed to the best advantage by the clerks, as competition was sharp, held them as interested spectators.

"Let us go out toward the bayou," said Antoine. They turned the first street. Quaint cottages began to line the way. Orange and lemon trees, climbing roses and the cape jessamine, brought from France, appeared above the pickets.

"Those higher houses must belong to the Government officials, do they not, Antoine? Or to the Spanish grandees. Ah, the sweet perfume of the roses. Does not the scent produce a magical spell upon you? I feel as if I were carried out of myself into an experience of a subtle nature—something that might have transpired in another existence."

"Do not rhapsodize, Louis, in this heat," said Antoine. "This reminds me of Annette and of home. Those pretty Creole girls are peeping through the lattice as if we were curiosities."

"Our costumes are not *a la Paris*," said Louis, taking off his skin cap, and viewing it in a critical manner. "Let us return. I must look for my uncle at any rate."

They retraced their steps and finally came to a broad open space.

"This," said Louis, "must be the Place d'Armes. The esplanade leads from this square," he said, scanning the doorways carefully, and referring to a slip in his hand. Presently he stopped before a grimy building, covered with a dingy stucco, parts of which had dropped off, showing

the bricks underneath. "Antoine, this must be
the place, though I think but little of it." He
dreamed not of the gold that changed hands here,
of the checks that were cashed, of the deep-laid
schemes for money-getting, for money-keeping,
that were hatched in the brain of his relative.

When Louis entered the low door, he found
his uncle half hidden behind an ancient desk,
with his head bent low over his accounts.

"Bon jour," cried Louis gayly.

"What! you here, Louis?" said Monsieur Perrine in astonished and rapid French. He had
met his nephew two years before in Baltimore.
Louis was the son of a much loved sister of Monsieur Perrine.

"This is my friend Antoine Beauvais."

"I knew your father. We were at the same
school. How is Monsieur Beauvais?"

"Thank you, in usual health," replied Antoine
respectfully.

"Here are the papers sent you by *le grandpere*," said Louis, taking a leather belt from his
person, and fumbling for the papers hidden
within its recesses.

"Ah, yes," said his uncle, looking them over
hastily. "This is right, and that—yes, I will

attend to the matter. Give yourself no further trouble."

Louis' face lighted up with a smile. He had wonderfully frank eyes. They expressed implicit confidence in the speaker, which was flattering to his companion and invariably pleased.

"You and your friend must come to the house to-morrow. The *tante* is absent to-day. I will see you there at five."

With proper thanks the two withdrew. As they passed out they brushed against some one about to enter.

"Pardon, Senor," said a musical voice, and a dark-eyed Spaniard stepped aside. This was Senor de Gonsalvo, who had a large speculation under consideration, which Louis' uncle was to manage.

"*Distingué*," said Louis to Antoine.

"Oui. One meets all sorts, Spanish grandees on one hand, and Canadian trappers on the other."

"We are the latter," said Louis.

"Trappers this side of Canada," said Antoine, mockingly.

Louis shrugged his shoulders; then a burning blush passed over his face. "I am a dog. The greatest of human characteristics belong to these Canadian trappers—courage indomitable, patient endurance in privation and suffering. They bore the burnt; you and I are feasting in their tracks. I were not a man should I disparage them." And his countenance filled with enthusiasm.

After a silence of some length, Louis exclaimed: "Antoine, the mail ship leaves tomorrow. So Francis Menard told me last night."

"I must then prepare my letter to the *pere* and Annette."

He looked so woebegone that Louis laughed heartily, and asked: "What is it, Antoine?"

"I am a fool when it comes to the pen, Louis. Ah, if I had been more attentive to Father Olivier's instructions! But to-morrow will be soon enough," he added, glad to postpone the dreaded undertaking.

That evening, wearied with a day that after all had been a little heavy on their hands, they sought outside diversion. Stepping warily over the treacherous walk, they met two female figures progressing slowly along the street. The one nearest to Antoine slipped and fell into a slimy puddle of water. Antoine, with native politeness, sprang forward to assist her to rise. As he lifted up the slight form, a negress held aloft a lantern and cried, "Ma'm'selle, Ma'm'-selle," and with excited ejaculations asked if she was injured.

The light of the lantern revealed to Antoine a face of exquisite beauty. The veil had fallen back, and soft eyes were raised to his in a dazed way.

"Thank you, I thank you, Monsieur. I have no injury," she murmured, and as she recovered her composure, she added in a sweet voice: "Come, Adele," and with dignity proceeded on her way.

Antoine was silent for so long a time that Louis turned his raillery upon him.

"Don't, Louis, I wish not to talk at present."

A vision was ever before Antoine's eyes of lovely, wondering eyes lifted to his, and he could not at once throw off their spell. In a short time he proposed to end their walk.

The next day, according to appointment, Antoine and Louis made their appearance at the residence of Monsieur Perrine. He was awaiting them. Madame Perrine received them kindly, and talked with vivacity of the voyage down the great river.

Antoine's heart leaped within him when through the open door a young girl entered the room carrying a handful of flowers.

"Ma'm'selle Leonie," said Monsieur Perrine.

She made a graceful courtesy to the young men. Antoine recognized the lovely countenance that had rested on his arm for a moment.

She was his *vis-a-vis* at the table. He summoned courage to look in her direction, and, catching inadvertently a glance from the dark eyes, he saw that the recognition was mutual. The young girl did not refer to the encounter, doubtless through timidity, for she sat modestly silent, while Monsieur and Madame Perrine conversed with their guests.

After the repast was finished, the company went into the garden. Cape jessamine and roses climbed the gallery. At the foot of the garden was a group of trees. Orange, lemon, cypress and laurel formed an attractive background.

A high palisade fence inclosed all and insured privacy. As the group dispersed Antoine found himself by the side of Leonie.

"Did Ma'm'selle suffer any injury from her accident last evening?" asked Antoine, in low tones.

"No, Monsieur Beauvais," said Leonie, blushing, "do not speak of it. I am humiliated to remember that awkward slip."

"No, Ma'm'selle Leonie," Antoine hastened to say, "it was the fault of the wretched pavement and the dark.

"Thank you, Monsieur. You are too polite to allow the truth. I should have been more watchful, but in reality I am not used to traveling there at that hour without some one else than Adele to accompany me." Antoine did not inquire, but Leonie continued to explain: "A near relative is very ill, and she detained me too long. I knew that Adele would scold," she said naively.

"Adele was very much frightened. She could not chatter fast enough in her anxiety," said Antoine laughing. He was watching his young companion with respectful admiration. Her beautiful eyes were shyly raised to his; her little hands toyed with a dark red rose that she carried. A delicious tremor filled his being as he thought: "What a lovely creature! I would this walk might last forever."

Madame Perrine turned back to speak with Leonie. Then the party lingered at the side of the lawn, where some rustic seats were placed.

Here they enjoyed the cool breeze after the heat of the day. The Spaniard whom they had seen at the office the day before was admitted through the gate by Adele. His manner of approach indicated that he was on very easy terms with the family. After introductions, Senor de Gonsalvo said: "I did have the pleasure of seeing your nephew yesterday, Monsieur Perrine."

"Ah, where was that?"

"We both tried to occupy the doorway at the same time," said the Spaniard, smiling, and showing a set of white teeth. "Do you make a long stay with us?"

"During a part of the summer, Senor."

"I shall have the pleasure of seeing you often. If I can serve you in any way, I would be very happy," he said affably.

"Thank you, Senor, you are very good."

Senor de Gonsalvo then addressed his remarks to Leonie. Antoine felt like throwing him over the picket and made a half start, then remembered where he was, and that he, Antoine, was the stranger, and not the Spaniard.

"We know very little of the town," said Antoine to Madame Perrine.

"It is very gay for the young men," she answered. "Balls and play the year round."

"Here are tickets for the grand fete next week," said Senor de Gonsalvo, producing the cards, and handing them to her with a bow.

"Ah, thank you, Senor." Then, turning toward her niece, "Leonie, let us go to the salon and listen to your song."

Leonie looked timidly at Antoine, but the request of the *tante* must be complied with.

Monsieur Perrine brought out a harp, upon which Leonie touched a few chords. She had been very carefully taught at the Ursuline convent. When the first bird-like tones issued from her throat, a hush fell upon the company. Antoine, with his deep love for music, listened in rapture to her song. Monsieur Perrine called for yet another. The color mounted in her cheeks at Antoine's evident admiration of her music. She wished to be excused, but her uncle would have a spirited French air.

Senor de Gonsalvo then sang in a rich tenor voice some love songs in his native tongue, the soft, musical voice blending in a dulcet strain with the accompaniment played by Leonie's deft fingers.

The evening ended with sprightly conversation.

It was with regret that Antoine and Louis bade adieu to Monsieur Perrine's family. Senor de Gonsalvo said at parting that he would have the pleasure of calling on the young strangers the next day.

This was the first of many happy evenings spent in Monsieur Perrine's home.

CHAPTER XIII.

THE whole city turned out to the fete. The esplanade was crowded. Antoine and Louis pushed their way through the throng, with Henri in their wake. The moving mass of French, Spaniards, Indians, mulattoes and negroes surged back and forth, according to the interest taken in especial sights. The military parade at the Place d'Armes would be the main attraction, but that was not to come off until eleven o'clock, so that there was much time yet to be disposed of.

"Wait, Antoine," said Henri, pointing to a group of negroes.

"What is it, Henri?"

"They are going to have the juba dance," answered Henri.

Two or three serious-looking Africans were sitting on some casks, clapping their hands and patting their knees with a sort of rude rhythm,

101

while several were going through the dance with such grotesque movements and fantastic steps as came to them with the inspiration of the moment. The number of the dancers would be increased from time to time as a bystander was seized with a magnetic spell which he could not resist, or one would drop out just as suddenly.

"Which one will hold out the longest?" asked Louis.

"I wager the old one with the gray hair. Take a louis?"

"No, the younger, whose favorite is the straight jump in the air, and a drop with both hands together."

The group broke up with a laugh as a Spanish sailor, with an overdose of the tafia, tried to join in with the others and put them out of time. More than one clenched fist helped him out of the way.

Leaving this scene, the friends walked down the street. In the cabaret, the Spaniards with song and guitar entertained themselves and the crowd who roughly jostled one another about the windows and doors. They made another round of the Place d'Armes, and arrived at the quaint Hotel de Ville. Glancing upward as they passed, Antoine saw Monsieur Perrine in the window of one of the offices. Leonie was standing at his side. From this position they would have a good view of the parade.

"Louis," said Antoine, "there is Monsieur Perrine."

"Ah, where?" asked Louis, looking about him.

"In the upper window, to the right."

As Louis raised his eyes Monsieur Perrine discovered the two friends, and he beckoned vigorously to them. Louis nodded to his uncle. They then forced their way through the jam at the entrance.

Monsieur Perrine was in a most amiable mood. The man of business was left in the grimy office, and he was as jubilant as a school boy on a holiday.

"Is there such beautiful weather on the Kaskaskia River?" asked Leonie, with a smile that Antoine thought bewitching indeed.

"Oui, Ma'm'selle. In our season of spring there are days that make one feel at peace with all mankind, when the sun shines warm out of a blue sky, and the white, fleecy clouds float lazily overhead. The trees are waving their green leaves to the gentle breeze, and birds trill forth their musical lays. The fields, too, are green, and there is a shimmer of light on either side as the lines of the rivers appear. If one is riding on his pony, over the 'common field,' he sees all this, and also the blue outline of the bluff."

"But you have cold, stormy winters, and rain, and deep mud—is it not so?"

"That is true, but this only makes us enjoy the season of which I speak the more," replied Antoine, "and before the winter of storm there is a season which is just like the dreamy unconsciousness which is not sleep, nor yet is one awake. And such are these days of which I tell you. The crops are sown and harvested. There is small need of more exertion. There is a haze in the atmosphere, which is blue in our Indian summer. The hills are dimly seen, as if far away. The leaves begin to fall, and presently the foliage is thinner, but the leaves are so many that at first the fallen ones are hardly missed. Later a few sharp touches, and the forest is one mass of gold and red and yellow. The setting sun will light up the bluffs on the east of our Kaskaskia River, and they are aflame."

"Then what?" she inquired.

"Then," said Antoine, smiling, "the whirr of

the quail is music in my ears, and the *couriers du bois* are abroad. The air is black with the wild fowl, and the crack of the rifle awakes the echoes of distant hills."

"Listen, Monsieur, there is the sound of fife and drum. The soldiers are coming."

The attention of all is then given to the review that is taking place in the open space below.

Before the party separated Leonie asked Antoine about the ball. "Do you and Louis think to be there?"

"Will you be present, Ma'm'selle?"

"That is the plan. My uncle has the tickets."

"We would not miss it for a great deal," said Antoine, resolving that nothing should prevent him from going if Leonie would be there.

"Louis," said M. Perrine, "I have examined the papers that you left with me. I will see you at the office in the morning. I wish to speak of some matters connected with them."

Louis promised to meet his uncle at the hour named.

"Shall we see you to-night at '*le grand bal*'?"

"Ah, indeed, yes, *mon oncle*."

"Louis," said M. Perrine, taking him aside, "you have made proper arrangements to appear in suitable costume? You must realize—"

Monsieur Perrine hesitated, and gave a little cough, as if clearing his throat. He knew that young men are high-spirited and will not always receive suggestions, even when needed.

"All that is fixed, *mon cher oncle*. We have talked the matter over with Senor de Gonsalvo. Is that satisfactory to you?"

"Entirely." And Monsieur Perrine appeared to be relieved.

"Adieu, then, my Louis, for a few hours."

CHAPTER XIV.

THE OLD MILL.

"ANNETTE," said Marie, one morning about three weeks after Antoine's departure, "Ma'm'-selle Somers has decided that we must make our sketches. Will you go?"

"Yes, if it be the pleasure of Ma'm'selle."

"I wish Antoine were here. How we shall miss him," continued Marie. "He is the life of such occasions."

"Why," inquired Annette, "are others to go?"

"Indeed, yes," replied Marie. "Do you think of a day just for sketching? It would be one long *ennui*," (tossing her head). "We are to have lunch by the stream, and perhaps a fish in the pond."

"Risden can take the provisions in the canoe. Jule might help him carry the things up the hill. Jule makes excellent coffee."

"The English lady would prefer tea, would she not?"

"No doubt that is true. Monsieur St. Gemme
will go, and—"

Marie looked embarrassed.

"And what, Marie?"

"There is a friend, or at least some one that
Monsieur met last year—an American gentleman.
He thinks of coming to our village to remain."

"How do you know? Have you met the
American?"

"Why—yes—I have."

"Marie," said Annette, sternly, "you seem to
have no end to your acquaintances." She added
sarcastically: "Pray does any one enter or leave
our village and you are not aware of it?"

"No, Annette, you needn't frown," retorted
Marie. "If I were you I would take the veil.
You care so little for the world or the people in
it."

"Marie, do not speak so lightly of *les relig-
ieuses*," said Annette, reprovingly.

"To explain," said Marie, changing the subject, "I was at Josephine's, and Monsieur St.
Gemme came to the house, bringing this stranger
with him. So, Annette, I could not well avoid
making his acquaintance. Besides, he is very
entertaining, for he has traveled much."

"What is the name of this favored and gifted one?" asked Annette, in the same sarcastic spirit.

"Monsieur Waring—Edgar Waring."

"Ah," was the only response to this information.

"Annette, I may tell Ma'm'selle that you are disposed to accompany us?"

"Pray, give my compliments to Ma'm'selle; I shall be pleased to go."

Marie left with a bright face. She had not mentioned that Baptiste was to be one of the party, for fear that Annette would peremptorily decline to go. "Why does she dislike him so? He is polite. Is it but her notion?"

The various individuals who were to join in the pleasure-seeking met at the ferry. Risden and Jule were dispatched with careful instructions as to their precious charge. "Be at the spring by the time we shall arrive," called St. Gemme as they took the oars.

After crossing the ferry our pedestrians followed the river. A two-mile walk would be a guarantee of a just and due appreciation of every dainty and sweetmeat that the cooks of the various families represented could devise.

Annette gave Marie a side glance of reproach

when she saw Baptiste among the expectant group. However, after the first salutations Baptiste devoted himself to Miss Somers, relieving her of the materials for drawing, and otherwise assisting her. This was a time when Baptiste could appear to advantage. Always neat and particular as to his dress, he felt especially well satisfied with himself this morning, and inwardly delighted that Annette had not remained at home. Nature had blessed him with a clearcut profile and a pair of bright, dark eyes, but lines of weakness and subtle cunning were about his mouth. There was not absolute wickedness, but under certain circumstances Baptiste might be able to accomplish much harm.

Edgar Waring walked with Josephine and Marie, while Annette was left with Monsieur St. Gemme. The stranger, about twenty-three years old, had a visible air of enterprise and pioneer spirit about him. Annette decided in his favor.

"Marie did not exaggerate as usual, in his case," she thought.

Waring was a tall blonde, with great, square shoulders and kindly blue eyes. He was very much interested in all that he saw, and asked innumerable questions about the people and the country, but in a way that did not offend.

Josephine, the sweetest and most devoted of mothers, joined in the conversation from time to time. She had come to-day to please Marie, who had coaxed her so prettily.

"Ah, here is a cart going to mill," said St. Gemme.

"Get in and ride," said Mr. Waring.

"Do; we will walk alongside."

"We shall need some poles for prods," laughed Baptiste.

The lazy oxen refused to hasten their pace. No urging, or prodding, or walking by the side or ahead on the part of the men, affected the animals in the least.

"Their activity cannot be aroused," said Baptiste, in a mock discouraged tone.

As a turn of the road brought them to a spring, Miss Somers exclaimed: "Now, here is the best point for a perspective. The ravine makes an inward curve. There is space along the ledge for a passage-way. The mill is in the foreground, and a great hill arises abruptly to our left. The brook is below us."

All agreed that this was the most desirable

point of view. Baptiste threw some Indian
blankets on the ground for the ladies.

"While we are not needed, and possibly not
wanted,"— said Monsieur St. Gemme.

"Chut," said Marie, "as if you of all people
were not wanted! Your presence is always in
request."

Monsieur St. Gemme laughed. "My presence
just now would be a luxury. It is not a
necessity."

"Come, Baptiste, where are the blacks? They
should have been ahead of us with the tackle
and provisions.

"Ah, here they are now," said Waring, as the
heads of the two appeared through the brush.

"Disputing, as usual," said St. Gemme.

"Risden would not agree with St. Peter himself," said Baptiste.

"Or Satan," said Monsieur St. Gemme, "and
he certainly will have his opportunity for that."

"Where is the bait, Jule?"

Jule looked blank.

"Did you forget?" asked his master, sternly.

Jule commenced in voluble French to apologize, to explain that he would, at once, procure
a great quantity.

"Jule, no delay," said Monsieur St. Gemme.
"See that you have it ready by the time we are
all at the pond."

"Oui, Monsieur." And he started off with
alacrity, and soon disappeared around the corner
of the mill. If his legs lagged then, no matter;
the day was before him.

Edgar Waring took Marie's sketch-book and
pretended to help her in making observations.
He insisted that the pencils were not in proper
condition, and consumed much time in preparing
them for use.

"Ma'm'selle, that is too heavy a stroke, I am
sure, quite sure."

"I think not, Monsieur."

"I will ask Miss Somers; she will confirm my
statement."

"Do not trouble, Monsieur."

"Ma'm'selle Marie," (Waring's French was
fair), "is that meant for a window or a door?"
he said, with great interest in his voice.

He continued his remarks until Miss Somers
despaired of getting any good work from Marie;
so she gave Monsieur St. Gemme an appealing
look, to go away with the young men. He answered by gathering up the long hickory poles
that served for rods.

"Come, Waring, we are losing our opportunity
with the minutes.   The fish will not bite after
ten o'clock."

"I leave you my encouragement," said Baptiste
to the young artists, bowing himself away.

The men followed in the wake of Jule, and
around to the dam, whence the water was carried to the wheel by modern aqueducts. Waring
burst into an exclamation of astonishment as the
beautiful sheet of water came into view.   It
was in a basin formed by the hills, and covering
perhaps forty acres.   The rounded points of the
hills, sloping abruptly to the water, made an
irregular outline of the entire circuit of shore.
Some groups of the young water willows showed
their heads above the surface, and resembled
miniature islands.   The forest covered the
slopes, and green moss made a thick carpet
about the roots of the trees.

"A jewel in the lap of—"

"Nature," suggested St. Gemme.

The fish proved to be eager, and the men
were soon absorbed in the exciting sport. Jule
surprised them by being at hand with the required bait.   He neglected to state that he had
bribed some small boys who were fishing on the

other side to share with him. The boys that came to mill would spend their time fishing while waiting their "turn" for a grind. The busy hum and whirr of the mill awoke the soft echoes among the hills.

The time passed unnoticed until Risden's voice rang out from the heights over them: "Jule, you Jule! Madame St. Gemme wants you dis minute, to make de coffee, you heah?"

A hearty laugh from the three men frightened away a poor fish that was trying to get the bait from Waring's hook.

"Tell Madame that Jule shall go immediately," called back Monsieur. "Go, Jule—do not keep Madame waiting. That also means," he added, addressing the other fishermen, "that we are to abandon this fascinating occupation, and appear in time to render what aid our united wisdom in woodcraft may prompt."

Waring and Baptiste were quite willing to rejoin the ladies. As they passed the mill it was shut down for the noon hour. The miller was leaning for the moment on the closed half door, regarding their approach.

"Did you have any luck, Monsieur St. Gemme?" he asked, looking curiously at the American.

"Thank you, yes, a pleasant day," responded St. Gemme.

Josephine and Marie were spreading the cloth on a great rock on the ledge, not far from the spring. Miss Somers was putting some finishing touches to the sketches. Annette was sitting alone under the shade of a great tree whose gnarled roots reached from one bank of the rivulet to the other, the earth washed out from under leaving them exposed. She was absorbed in her own thoughts. Waring and Baptiste enlisted in the service of Josephine and Marie. The latter was free and graceful in her movements as a young fawn.

"She is in her native element here in the woods," thought Waring.

Monsieur St. Gemme sat down by Annette. He examined her paper in friendly criticism. "Your eyes are true, Annette," he said kindly. A pleased look filled her countenance. "But that is the case in another sense," he said gravely.

"What do you mean, Monsieur?"

"I mean that when the nature is true, the heart is true to all its obligations in life. Annette," he asked after a silence, "is Monsieur

Beauvais in his usual health this spring?"

"Why do you ask?" she said, after a moment.

If Annette was unconscious of any change, he disliked to call her attention to it, or to arouse unnecessary uneasiness. The scene on the day before Antoine left still haunted him. He felt apprehension on account of Monsieur Beauvais. Apparently forgetful of his question, he said:

"Annette, now that Antoine is away, should anything occur—that is, should you have need, do not fail to apprise me, that I may come to your assistance. Promise me that."

She looked at him gratefully. The moisture came into her eyes, and she felt an impulse to tell him of the dread that filled her heart; but this was not a fitting time or place, so she restrained her feelings, and answered him quietly:

"I will, Monsieur."

He gazed into those large and expressive eyes. The innocent soul of a young girl looked forth. Whatever he, with his wider experience, read therein, he made no sign, but said:

"I am satisfied. Rest assured that whatever I may be able to do for Monsieur Beauvais or his family will be deemed a privilege."

Jule was now ready with his share of the feast,

broiled fish and hot coffee. Monsieur St. Gemme
and Annette joined the others at their repast.
St. Gemme sat down by his wife to do the
honors, and dispensed the courtesies of the table
in a genial manner. In any situation requiring
tact he was at his best. Repartee flew fast between Marie and the young men. Even Annette
ventured a few lively sallies, inspired by the
mirth of the others.

"What shall we do with the remaining time
at our disposal?" asked Miss Somers in her very
precise way, after the lunch had been partaken
of most generously.

"I think we must ask Marie," said Monsieur
St. Gemme, turning to her. "She is the director
general."

"Then," said Marie, gayly, "we will first go to
the spring and lave our fingers," holding hers up
and looking at them ruefully. "Fricasseed
chicken will leave its marks. I will lead the
way."

Baptiste dipped up the pure, sparkling water
with a gourd and poured it over Marie's pretty
pink fingers, at the same time offering her a
spotless *mouchoir* for her use.

"Baptiste, as you are so kind I will spread

this over a bush to dry, and we can find it on
our return."

Madame St. Gemme proposed that they should
climb the hill overlooking the shimmering pond
and find a greensward where they could rest and
tell stories.

"You begin, Ma'm'selle," said Marie, panting
for breath, when they reached the top.   Tell us
about your home in England.

This was a subject near to Miss Somers' heart,
and she graphically described the scenes amid
which she had passed her girlhood.

"Now, Monsieur Waring next."

Waring told of Claiborne's rebellion and the
early persecution of Catholics in many lands—
tales that he had heard around his mother's knees
when but a lad.

Baptiste told of a hunting expedition in which
he and Antoine and others had engaged. A
blinding storm of snow and sleet had come upon
them in the prairie, lasting two days. They had
thought that to perish with cold or to become
food for the wolves was their inevitable fate.

"Monsieur St. Gemme, tell us about the Indian
raid on Paget's Mill," coaxed Marie.

CHAPTER XV.

"AH, that is an old story. Are you not yet tired of it?"

"No, and Monsieur Waring has not yet heard the account."

"Proceed," said Waring, in an interested manner. "I wish to hear it, I must hear it," he added, looking at Marie.

"There is not much to tell," said St. Gemme. "Monsieur Paget recognized the value of the location for a mill site. No doubt he thought only of the business suitability, and not of the beauty of the place. Yet what more fitting spot could have been found for the ideal miller? There must always be more or less of the romantic interest attached to the surroundings of a mill, water being the first necessity, and the vegetation that follows the course of the stream. Often the broken contour of the ground adds a wild picturesqueness to the situation."

"And such is true of this particular site," said Marie, waving her hand toward the mill below them.

"This place was at a convenient distance from the village, the water-power to hand. The great problem with the first settlers was to get their corn ground. The old-fashioned horse mills were inadequate to supply the demand. There was plenty of rock in these bluffs. Taking advantage of this fact, Monsieur Paget erected a substantial structure, and engaged in the manufacture of flour for the New Orleans market. That was about the year 1765. The country was not secure from Indian depredations at that time, and all who settled away from the village underwent this great risk. The Kaskaskia Indians themselves (you can see the remnants of the Illinois, the Mitchgannies and the Kaskaskias on the outskirts of our village) remained in order to have the protection of the whites from their enemies, the Northern warlike tribes. One day Monsieur Paget and his negroes were surprised by a band of the Kickapoos, a most cunning and savage lot of warriors. One negro alone escaped to carry the word to the village. When the indignant pioneers reached the mill, they found it the scene of a most horrible massacre. The negroes had been butchered, and the body of Paget cut to pieces, and his head thrown into the hopper."

"It was the work of fiends," said Miss Somers. "I shudder to think of it."

"And they, too, are members of the human family! Bah, they are only brutes," said Waring. "Is the country free now from Indian raids about here?"

"Yes, but you must remember," said St. Gemme, "that we are yet upon the frontier."

"It is hard to believe that when I find so much wealth and fashion where I expected to find naught but a wilderness."

"We are old," said St. Gemme. "Pittsburgh was not thought of, Nouvelle Orleans did not exist, but we were a considerable town."

"When does your history commence?"

"From 1680 to 1686," answered St. Gemme.

"You are like a bee-hive now with your floating population," said Waring.

Annette frowned a little at this remark. "The mill was then abandoned, was it not, Monsieur?" she asked.

"Yes, for many years the place was avoided,

especially by the superstitious, who would hear the yells of the Indians and the shouts of the poor negroes in imagination. The building crumbled until only the walls remained."

"When did General Edgar come into possession?" asked Marie.

"In 1796 this tract came into his hands. He repaired the mill and the dam and did a thriving business for a number of years. The mill now is only run occasionally. Madame Edgar and a negress named Dice—Aunt Dice they called her—planted those cottonwood trees when the dam was repaired."

"They are in what the Dissenters would call 'good and regular standing,'" laughed Waring.

"Hush," said Miss Somers, "don't be irreverent."

They arose at this remark and wended their way down the hill.

"Baptiste," said Waring, "what say you? Let us set the mark and have a trial of skill."

"Very well," he answered.

The party gathered at the ravine to decide upon a mark.

"Here," said Waring, taking a letter with a broken seal out of his pocket. He put the letter in the fork of a small tree a few yards distant.

"The paper will give way," cried Baptiste.

"Can't," said Waring, laconically; "it is against the bark."

"Lead," said Monsieur St. Gemme, as they brought their long-barreled pistols to bear upon the mark. Baptiste took aim, but missed the center. Then Waring took his turn, going inside of Baptiste's shot.

"Fire," said Waring.

"No," said St. Gemme, "I'll wait."

"Go on."

Baptiste and Waring punctured the paper repeatedly, but failed of the center.

"Annette," said St. Gemme, turning to her, "do you wish to try your sight?"

To his surprise she answered, "Yes."

She took aim and fired. The shot made the exact center.

"Mere accident," she said, "for it is my first trial."

"I can cut the edge," said St. Gemme. Baptiste and Waring took a wager. Monsieur St. Gemme took aim and was as good as his word, as the ragged edge of the center shot showed to be the case. Waring regarded him with admiration.

"Ah, you did not know that Monsieur St. Gemme is the best shot in the country. The Indians knew it during the war of 1812," said Baptiste. "Annette," he continued, when Waring and St. Gemme became absorbed in a discussion of events following that war, "let us climb the ridge yonder, and see the village."

Annette wished to refuse. "Marie must come too," she said, "or Ma'm'selle Somers."

But the others were too tired. Madame St. Gemme, in her good nature, finally agreed to the proposition. But when nearly at the top of the ledge she declared herself exhausted, and said she would wait while they gained the highest point for the view. She seated herself on a bare brown rock to await their return.

"It is magnificent," said Annette, her eyes glowing at the prospect before her.

"Annette," said Baptiste, "has the day been full of pleasure to you? Have you had a happy time?"

"I have been very happy, Baptiste. Why do you ask?" She was in a mood to feel kindly toward the whole world.

Baptiste resolved to take advantage of the moment. "Because there is nothing that pleases me so much as to see you happy. I would always have you happy, if I could. Why do you avoid me so? You may know that the wish to· make you my wife is my greatest desire on earth. Our parents have favored the idea."

"Baptiste," said Annette, indignantly, "is this the reason why you have brought me here? You might have spared yourself this trouble. You have long known the nature of my feelings toward you."

"Wait, Annette; you may change," he said imploringly.

"I shall never change," she said passionately. "I do not wish to change. You shall not speak to me of such things again."

"Then, Annette, there must be some one else, for young girls will listen to talk of love until the end of time. To most it is only sweet music to their ears."

A quick blush crimsoned her face and an angry light burned in her eyes.

"No, Baptiste, there is no one else," but her voice trembled in spite of her efforts to control her anger and dislike.

"Annette,"—and he took a step toward her, he in turn becoming angry at her indifference,

—"if there is any one else, I shall move heaven and earth to find who it is." He muttered threats, but Annette turned away from him and ran down the path. She knew, however, that she had that moment changed her lover into an enemy.

Madame St. Gemme said: "It is quite time to return to the village. You and Baptiste were a long time viewing old 'Kaskia."

Annette murmured some reply, with an averted face. She kept close to Miss Somers on the homeward tramp, excluding herself from the gay talk of those in advance. Risden and Jule had packed the hampers and had gone shortly after lunch.

CHAPTER XVI.

LE GRAND BAL.

ANTOINE and Louis with laugh and jest prepared to attend the ball with which the fete was to end. They viewed each other with congratulation and some admiration. The change produced by the habiliments which, guided by Senor de Gonsalvo's irreproachable taste, they had provided for the occasion, was amazing to them. The famous beauties of whom they had heard would doubtless single them out for especial favor, they laughingly assured themselves. Antoine was not at all disturbed at the thought of meeting the grandees of the town, for his one gift was an ease and charm of manner that would adapt itself to such a company.

Louis felt more trepidation. But Monsieur Perrine and his kind wife would be there, and he could take refuge in their company. At the time appointed Senor de Gonsalvo called for them on his way. He was richly dressed. The two

friends felt suddenly as if they were far removed
into the background, as at the entrance he saluted
them with a graceful wave of the hand.

"Pardon, but I am a few moments late, I fear."

"It is of no consequence, Senor," they exclaimed.

"If it is your pleasure we will proceed to the
ball-room."

Antoine and Louis were quite in sympathy
with this proposal. They had in reality been
consumed with impatience, notwithstanding Antoine's polite response to the Senor's apology.

The indulgent moon made plain their route,
and hidden traps in the walk were not dreaded
as on the night of the previous week. Men and
women in gala costume thronged the streets,
bent upon entertainment of various kinds. Antoine's spirits were light and in full keeping with
the hilarity about him. In anticipation he was
already at the dance, with Leonie as his light-
footed partner. Monsieur Perrine's party had
not arrived, much to his disappointment. However, the dancing had not yet commenced. Gay
groups were scattered about the hall—elegantly
dressed women and young girls with sleepy,
veiled eyes that presently would expand with

excitement and shine and sparkle like stars.

"Senor de Gonsalvo is a favorite, see," whispered Louis.

"It seems so. The *grandes dames* are smiling on him."

"He is rich and is descended from a family of rank," said Louis.

"There are five debutantes, just from finishing touches at the Ursuline, Madame Perrine told me."

"A worldly and striking contrast to their past, then," said Antoine. His eyes were roving. They were guarding the approach, that Leonie might not enter unobserved of him.

Senor de Gonsalvo came up to them. "I must have the happiness of presenting you as partner for some of the beautiful ladies."

So after all Antoine was on the floor dancing when Leonie arrived with her uncle and aunt. He felt his heart give one great bound. Then, strange to relate, he was all devotion to his partner, who afterwards said to the *grande dame*, her mother: "He has the most charming manners, this young Kaskaskian. Who is he, mamma?"

"I know not, *ma cherie*. It is all right, I doubt

not. Senor de Gonsalvo may tell you." And she continued her gossip with her neighbor.

Antoine and Louis soon joined the coterie about Monsieur Perrine and Madame.

Antoine, after the usual compliments were exchanged, asked permission to lead Leonie out upon the floor.

Louis' shyness had vanished as he entered the brilliantly lighted apartment, where scores of candles in their silver sconces shed luster over the scene. Antoine danced as he had never danced before. Leonie tripped lightly by his side. Madame Perrine smiled as she watched the young couple, so engrossed in their own pleasure, and totally unconscious of others. Senor de Gonsalvo gave a casual glance in their direction. If he observed their devotion he merely drew his brows together and turned away as if it was a matter of no importance, and gave them no further attention. Antoine spent as much time in Leonie's company as he thought in accordance with good taste. When at last the gray dawn was breaking in the east, and the candles had burned down to their sockets, the dancers began to give way.

"It is by far the most delightful ball I ever

attended," said Antoine to Leonie at parting.

"And I," said she, smiling sweetly upon him. Her drapery of tulle and silk was crushed by the exercise, and most of the rosebuds with which her costume was decorated had fallen off, but Antoine did not care for these minor points.

Madame Perrine smothered a yawn, and tapped Leonie on the shoulder with her elaborate fan.

"Come, come; it is high time we old people were in bed, and young eyes, too, need sleep, if I mistake not. Adieu, Monsieur; we shall have the pleasure of seeing you? Do not let too long a time pass by," she said to Antoine.

"Thank you, Madame. I shall be only too happy to avail myself of your permission."

This ball was the first of many festive gatherings attended by Louis and Antoine. They were known to represent families of wealth. Time flew by rapidly in this gay circle. Louis noted with some anxiety a dormant passion for play aroused in Antoine. Was this fashionable pastime of the day going to prove his ruin? Day and night men sat by the gaming-table trying to supply their never satiated appetite.

Louis played occasionally. When he saw its hold upon Antoine he tried to fill in the time in other ways. The growing interest in Leonie was an aid to Louis' plans, and he furthered this interest in every way. The memory of those hours of indescribable delight passed in the home of Monsieur Perrine returned again and again in the gloom that came to Antoine in after years.

Very often they would have tea in the sheltered garden. Bright and animated conversation would ensue. The annoying feature to Antoine was Senor de Gonsalvo's presence at these times. He did not usurp Leonie's society, however, but would converse often with Monsieur Perrine or Madame. They left Antoine free to be with Leonie. Strolling in the rose walks, the young people would exchange experiences, their unimportant thoughts and their views of life as it appeared to their youthful fancy.

"Shall we have music?" Monsieur Perrine would ask.

"Most certainly," the Senor would respond. "Will Ma'm'selle Leonie sing for us? Is the cold in her throat quite recovered?"

"I thank you, Senor, I am but slightly hoarse."

"The Senor will accompany on the guitar?" Antoine would inquire.

Then would follow a merry round, in which Leonie's clear soprano, the Spaniard's soft tenor and the fine bass voice of Louis would unite in harmony.

Does sorrow press as heavily and are the stings of grief as severe under the sunny skies as in our northern clime of ice and snow? Antoine, in all the confidence of youth, sought Monsieur Perrine in his office, one morning before the business of the day began to surge in and out through the low doorway. Monsieur Perrine waited for him to state his errand. Antoine's throat was a little husky, but, gazing straight into the shrewd face that was intent upon a sharp trade that day, he said:

"Monsieur Perrine, you must have seen that I am deeply interested in your niece, Mademoiselle Leonie. I ask your permission to address her with a view to making her my wife."

A slight, a very slight trace of a smile hovered about Monsieur Perrine's dry lips. "Have you apprised Ma'm'selle of this?" he asked.

"No, Monsieur, certainly not before I had spoken with you, though, no doubt, Ma'm'selle is not blind. She may have read my heart."

"It is well. I have made other arrangements for Ma'm'selle Leonie."

Antoine looked confounded and somewhat foolish. "Does—Ma'm'selle Leonie—know of these arrangements?"

"No, Ma'm'selle is very young yet. We thought best not to speak to her of them until another year had passed."

Antoine took his leave of Monsieur Perrine— he hardly knew in what manner. In reflecting afterward he hoped that he had been respectful. He walked the streets for hours. At one time he discovered that he had followed the bayou a long distance. He looked at the sluggish waters. "Such will life be to me in the future." He stopped and turned back. "I must see Leonie," he cried to himself. A miserable pain was tugging at his heart. It clung to him persistently through the long day. It was a welcome thought that Menard was preparing to return to Kaskas-kia. Did he think that he could leave that subtle pain behind?

At the last meeting in Monsieur Perrine's house he saw that it was quietly being managed so that he and Leonie should have no private talk. Leonie's glance followed him inquiringly. Her eyes were heavy, and there was a wan look upon her face. "Was this on account of his

absenting himself for the past several days?
How could he ascertain the truth in the
matter?"

"Ma'm'selle Leonie," he said boldly at parting, "may I have the rose you carry in your
hand, to keep as a reminder of the young rose
I leave blooming in Monsieur Perrine's home?"

She blushed and handed him the flower. His
eyes were eloquent as he thanked her. Monsieur Perrine could not prevent that expressive
language which told far more than the spoken
word.

Antoine and Louis departed after the message
for friends in old Kaskaskia had been stated and
restated over and over again. As Adele attended
them to the gate, Antoine slipped a note into
her hand.

"It is for your mistress, Mademoiselle Leonie."

"She shall have it, Monsieur," said Adele.

Antoine thought that he might trust her, as
she had regarded him with special favor since
the night of the accident.

In the note he informed Leonie of the attach-
ment she had inspired in him, but owing to
reasons that were beyond his control he could
not address her. He would have to carry a

broken heart through life with him, but there
was one thing that he would ask, and that was,
should she ever find herself in trouble and need
his assistance, he would fly to her relief—would
she write for him?

Louis decided to remain in the city, as the
business on which he had come was not yet
completed. Antoine did not confide in Louis
his heart affair. He possessed something of his
father's reserve in such matters, while very frank
in the other affairs of life.

CHAPTER XVII.

THE RETURN.

"WHERE is Henri?"

"Why, don't you know?" said one of the voyageurs.

"No," said Antoine, beginning to feel alarmed.

The man laughed. "To tell the truth, he is safe for the present."

"What do you mean?" said Antoine, angrily. "If you have anything to say tell it."

"Some of those Spaniards were after him to get their fun. Henri boasts that he could drink. They wager him he could not drink one of tafia to their four, their ten. He took them, and with their bad French and his poor stock of Spanish I know not what would have been the end. One of our voyageurs came along and brought him too."

"Where is he now?" demanded Antoine.

"The last I knew, he is in the lock-up. Jacques was bringing him to the river, when they

138

passed a bird man on the corner. Henri was not clear, and he thought the birds better to be free than in the cage, so he opened the door of the cage."

"The fool!" muttered Antoine.

"The seller raised a big cry. The crowd and the boys they take it up, and have a big melée. The grand officials say that Henri has offended against the peace. They will keep him for a while."

Antoine knew not what to do in this strait. He awaited Francis Menard's coming with impatience. Menard frowned when he heard the circumstances; then a thought occurred to him.

"Wait till night," he said; "we'll have to take him out; for we can't wait weeks for them to take up his case. They are slow. Attention, voyageurs." He passed the word to be on hand promptly, at night. "I have a soft job for you."

At midnight he marshalled his forces, and, having left a swivel or two to protect the bateau, he marched his men to the calaboose. He drew them up in line and called out in loud French:

"I demand this prisoner, and the first man that interferes will be shot."

At a signal the guards were covered, and they dared not interpose. Having rescued his prize, he marched to the river, followed by the cheers of the crowd that is always on hand on such occasions, springing up from who knows where.

"Come, move on before the rascals have a chance to retaliate." The men took to the oars in haste.

"Henri, you ugly beast, to put the Capitaine to all this trouble, and maybe danger," reproached Antoine.

"The lad was hardly worth it, but I promised Monsieur Beauvais to return his son. Antoine would not have gone without Henri," said Menard dryly.

The night was calm and dark, save for the star-light. The men were fresh and rowed steadily until the dawn broke. Then the Capitaine ordered them to halt. He took off his red cap and bared his brow to the fresh, life-giving air. Coffee and bacon had been given to the men, who were tired with their long pull.

"Voyageurs, rest for the next two hours."

A valuable cargo was on board, worth many thousands of dollars.

"What do you carry, Capitaine?" said Antoine, sleepily, as he stretched himself out to rest.

"Provisions for William Morrison's big trade. I took up a cargo for Pierre last time. I hope those molasses kegs won't leak this time."

Henri, who wished to atone for his escapade of yesterday, took his turn manfully at the cordelle.

By means of pulling, rowing and pushing along the banks with great poles the bateau was gaining slowly. Hundreds of miles were to be traversed in this laborious manner. The men at the cordelle either swam the shallow streams or crossed in canoes. Sometimes the cordelle was wound around a large tree and worked upon the principle of the windlass to draw the heavy cargo up stream. The first brick house in Kaskaskia was built of bricks brought down the Ohio River and taken up the Mississippi in flatboats, a slow and tedious process.

They had been out six weeks, when one day at noon the sky began to darken and thick clouds were charging across the heavens. A streak of yellow light shone in the southwest. The voyageurs were commencing to show signs of fear. Ominous sounds were heard.

"Get a sail ready," ordered the Capitaine. He stood at the helm, brave and intrepid, with calm eyes gazing at the approaching storm.

"There will be a hurricane," said Antoine, as a funnel-shaped cloud suddenly separated into several finger-like divisions, that dipped and rose alternately, as it swept along the bend of the river.

"I tell you it is too much of a risk this time, Capitaine," shouted one of the voyageurs with forbidding looks. Menard called him a dog. The water was dark and sullen. The waves, started up by the wind, broke into lines of white foam, the bateau violently rocking with their force.

Menard seemed to have within his nature a power that was called out by a disturbance of the elements. He stood immovable at the rudder, a striking figure in his red cap and great capote.

There was a sudden roar; the clouds assumed a greenish cast, lifted, and rushed overhead in the line of the bluffs on the right. Forest trees were torn up by the roots, and the large branches were sent tumbling along before the mighty force of the whirlwind. Birds were blown out

of their nests and drowned in the torrents of rain
that accompanied the outburst. The sails taking
the outer edge of the wind, the bateau swept
along at a tremendous pace. Antoine and
Henri held their breath, expecting every moment
to be dashed into eternity. A few hours of
drenching rain, and then, as they were rounding
an island, a great stretch of rich bottom land on
one side and high bluffs on the other, the sun
shone out at the setting and enveloped them in
a golden mist in which the scene was a fairy-
land.

That night as they gathered about the blazing
camp-fire Antoine said with a shiver, "I am
much chilled," warming his hands in the blaze.

"Here," said Henri, "take this," handing him
a cup of black coffee with spirits in it,

The morning found Antoine feverish, and not
like himself, but drooping and dull.

"You must take this powder, Antoine. The
Capitaine says it does you good."

But Antoine shook his head impatiently. "I
of all people ought to bear a little wetting.
What is that to me?"

"The Capitaine say you shall, Antoine. You
be sick a long time, and I know you not like
that, Antoine."

But Antoine refused the medicine. He thought it a preposterous idea. But in a few days the fever continued to rise rapidly, Antoine moaning as if in great pain. Francis Menard peremptorily administered the powders. A number of weary, tedious weeks followed. Antoine fretted under this, to him, new experience. His fine health and a system inured to exposure had made him invulnerable, he had supposed, to disease. Henri proved himself an invaluable nurse. He listened to Antoine's raving during the progress of the fever. Antoine seemed to be living over again the scenes in New Orleans. "Leonie" was so often on his tongue that Henri felt a jealous pang for fear that Antoine might go to New Orleans to live. "And all for that Ma'm'selle," thought he. Snatches of songs that Antoine had learned while there would fall from his lips. Some dark-eyed stranger seemed to annoy him. "Leonie," he cried, starting up, "you would not surely—not to him." Then the remainder of the sentence died away on his lips. "Not another game to-night," he would cry. "I have no stake. His voice is soft and sweet, and he sings songs only of love. I know not his words, but his glances tell me it is so."

"Antoine, Antoine!" Henri would say. "It is nothing. You are with Henri. We are going home, home, Antoine."

"Home," he repeated vacantly, and then relapsed into his wanderings.

Henri was in despair. "What will Monsieur Beauvais and Annette—Annette with her great eyes—what—if anything happens to Antoine?"

Francis Menard looked grave these days. "Watch him closely, lad. We must get him back to old 'Kaskia."

Antoine's constitution finally brought him out of the attack. Then came long days of convalescence. The season was changing during the slow progress toward the north. The October days were a little sharp, and the notes of the wild duck were heard. Antoine felt his pulses leap with the instinct of the hunter. One day, after his strength had partially come back to him, he said:

"Come, Henri, bring the guns. Let's try for some birds over there in the swamp."

"Don't go beyond call," said Menard warningly. They made a detour and came out on a small lake, the haunt of wild ducks. Antoine made several successful shots. Henri secured the game and carried back to camp a bunch of fowl with glossy black feathers. The wings were tipped with blue and green, and so were the neck and head.

"Antoine, see there," said Henri, pointing to the top boughs of a tall tree. Antoine looked up. He saw two Indian coffins made of logs hewn out neatly. In them had been placed the dead, awaiting the return of the band, when the remains would be taken to the burying-ground of the tribe.

Antoine turned away quickly. He would usually have been indifferent to a sight with which he had become familiar on former tramps. Now the new life was coming through his veins, and he shuddered at this reminder of dissolution. Life was inexpressively dear to him. He felt that he would not live to be *too old*. He was beginning to hope that the year might bring some turn in his fortunes, and that Leonie would yet become his wife. He knew not how it was to be brought about as yet, but time would reveal to him how to proceed. A halloo from camp hastened their footsteps.

The remaining weeks of the voyage passed without incident. When within a day's journey from the village, Henri and one of the crew were dispatched in a canoe, to inform their friends of the near approach of the voyageurs. As the bateau rounded the last curve, they saw that the banks were crowded with villagers—merchants, old men and young, matrons and young girls— merry figures in capote with handkerchief tied on head, or in hunting shirt and leggings of dressed deer-skin, with the skin of prairie wolf for cap. The red glow of the setting sun back of the village made it stand out in bold relief. The silvery chimes of the bell floated over the water. The familiar sight and sound thrilled Antoine's heart. He hastened ashore, expecting to meet his father and Annette, the first to welcome him. Risden and Jule were there.

"How is you, Antoine?" said Risden, his eyes shining.

"Well, but, Risden, where are my father and Annette?"

"The Monsieur not feeling strong—dat is, not right strong. He sent Risden to say he waitin' for you at de house "

Antoine felt a strange depression at this end of his long and eventful journey.

CHAPTER XVIII.

THE FRONTIER.

WARING was undecided as to his location. He wished to have a long talk with Vital St. Gemme as to the prospective advantages should he con· clude to remain in Kaskaskia. He walked down the street to St. Gemme's office, or rather to a room that was occupied by several individuals for various uses.

The desk stood in one corner. St. Gemme was busy examining some records, but laid them aside in order to give his attention to Waring. "Monsieur, I think you could not do better. You perceive the situation. The country is in a transition state. We shall doubtless be a State before many months."

"Trade certainly is active, I admit that," said Waring.

"Where will you find a more brilliant bar?" asked St. Gemme. "Here is young Kane, who is fast becoming famous, Nathaniel Pope, Baker,

John Scott; Thomas Reynolds is often here, and other talented lawyers."

"Kane tells me that he wants a schoolmate of his, Sidney Breese, to locate here. He says that the young man's ability is of the highest order."

"That is what we want—leading talent. Then is the country certain to advance."

"Too much talent, possibly, for me," laughed Waring. "What show will I have when there are so many bright lights to eclipse me? Seriously, I had intended to examine other points of the frontier as to suitability in carrying out my plans. I trust I may have at least a useful career."

Waring's manly tones and his sincere, earnest manner won St. Gemme's admiration.

"I have need to go to Cahokia," said St. Gemme, "and thence to Peoria, in order to examine certain papers in regard to grants. Do you come, and then you may know more of the country."

Waring thought a moment. "So I will. Just the thing."

The third day from that, fully equipped for the hardships of the long ride, they started on the trail leading to Cahokia.   Late in the evening they came to French Village, a neat little settlement near a large eminence.

"See that mound," said Monsieur St. Gemme. "That is called Big Mound.   A few years ago an order of monks were established there.   They were known as the 'Monks of La Trappe.'"

"Where are they now?"

"Oh, they moved away in 1813."

"How did they ever drift out into this wilderness?"

"I know not.   They were vowed to celibacy and to silence.   I have spoken to a number of them, but they were as silent as the grave to me. No woman could walk on their premises.   If any did so by accident, their tracks would immediately be swept away with aversion."

This remark suggested a thought to Waring.

"Marie is a graceful little creature, Monsieur St. Gemme—a contrast indeed to Ma'm'selle Beauvais.   The latter is cold even to *hauteur*, while Marie is all life and sparkle."

"The two have been warmly attached since childhood."

"Is Marie an orphan?   From what was said I inferred as much."   .

"Oh, no. Ma'm'selle Beauvais' mother died in childbirth. Madame Dubreil is in France. Marie is with her uncle, Madame's brother. The child has a tender heart. Her devotion to Annette Beauvais would prove that."

"I do not admire those proud and self-reliant natures," said Waring. A vision came to him of red, pouting lips, eyes demure, the next minute flashing saucy glances at him. He knew a little creature that to take under his protection would henceforth be an object to work for.

St. Gemme observed Waring closely as they cantered along in silence. "If Madame Dubreil were here," he thought, "she could manage this affair properly. It would not be a bad match. Waring, with his energy and talent, will succeed. Besides, Marie will have some property of her own. What a great fellow he is."

Monsieur St. Gemme was only of medium height, but of elegant figure. Waring was a man of fine proportions. His complexion was as fair as a girl's, but sun and wind would change that. His eyes were fearless in their expression. The distance betweeen points where they stoped for rest and refreshment was beguiled by stories of frontier life.

"Three years ago," said St. Gemme, "we could not have ridden as carelessly as we have to-day. Over there," (waving his hand in the direction of Hill Fort,) "near the present town of Greenville, occurred a most peculiar encounter between one intrepid soldier and three Indians. A company of rangers under Captain Owens started at daybreak to reconnoiter, when they fell into an ambush of the Indians. One of the soldiers, Higgins, was an extremely large man. He called to his companion to 'come on.' The man cried out that he was hit; he tried to mount, but his steed became frightened and ran. 'Limp on,' cried Higgins, 'I will protect you." His companion did crawl through the grass and reached the fort, while Higgins was left to battle with the three. One Indian was as large a man as Higgins. Higgins had been wounded, but did not know it in his excitement. He reloaded and fired; so did the two smaller Indians. Higgins fell, but was on his feet with his loaded gun. The large Indian must have believed the gun to be empty, or he would not have rushed on to his death. This enraged the other two. They rushed at Higgins furiously with tomahawks and spears, and nearly knocked him down

THE KANE HOME ON THE EAST BLUFFS.

FROM A PHOTO IN 1883.

by throwing the tomahawks at his head. But
the dauntless soldier pulled himself up by the
spear which one of the Indians presented to his
heart. He took his gun and crushed the brain
of the Indian, but the blow broke the stock.
There was now but one savage left to continue
the fight with the nearly exhausted soldier.
This happened within sight of the fort. One
woman became excited, and, mounting her horse,
said she couldn't stand by and see so brave a
man murdered. The men would not see a
woman go alone, and followed her. At their
approach the Indian fled."

"What became of Higgins?" asked Waring.

"He had fainted from loss of blood. They
found him mangled and nearly torn to pieces."

"Did he recover?"

"Yes, and lives near Vandalia. The wonderful
strength and endurance of the man is almost
without parallel."

"You were active in the campaign, Monsieur?"

"I saw some service," said St. Gemme,
modestly.

Waring had heard that Monsieur St. Gemme
was foremost in a number of engagements to
protect the settlement. He was cool and intrep-

id. The Indians dreaded his fire, for he was known among them as one who never missed his man.

"Monsieur Waring, I hope you may never have to enter into border warfare. The details are terrible and sickening. You who dwell in Eastern cities do not realize the ghastly scenes through which we have passed that this vast country might be preserved and held in trust for future generations."

"Do you not remember that the coast has passed through the same fire of conflict?" said Waring.

When in course of time the village of the Peorias was before them, St. Gemme said: "Here you see the effects of their late struggles. Capt. Craig was not content with forcing the villagers to remove to another site, but further satisfied his revenge by firing some of their best houses. Monsieur Le Croix—you have heard me mention him—was in Canada at the time. His fine home was one that fed the flames."

CHAPTER XIX.

THE CEDAR CHEST.

Miss Somers walked rapidly toward the Beauvais mansion, one morning about three weeks after the day at the old mill. There was no cause for haste, only that this was Miss Somers' natural gait. She proceeded by a series of jerks. She did not walk well for an Englishwoman. One would have thought the languor of the climate would have taken the spring out of her step by this time.

Rose opened the door.

"Is Annette at home, Rose?"

"I t'ink she is. I t'ink she is fixin' up the rose-bush in the garden. Walk roun' da, Miss Somers, or will you speak with Monsieur 'fore you see Annette?"

"Thank you. Is Monsieur Beauvais quite well?"

Rose shook her head and whispered confidentially: "Hush, honey, dey t'inks he is,

but Ise know better.   I dassen't speak of it to
Annette; she won't listen.   I is uneasy—I is,
indeed."

"I think your fears are groundless, Rose.   I
will not disturb Monsieur Beauvais, but go
directly to the garden."

"Dey's nothing serious yet, Miss Somers.   I
must speak of it to some one.   'Pears like it
must come off my mind.   But he does act a
little strange dese days.   He does for sure, Miss
Somers."

"Never mind, Rose, it will be all right.   Say
nothing of this to any one else," said Miss
Somers, as she hastened away.   She did not
wish to discuss family affairs with a servant.

Annette was attempting to fasten a rose that
had escaped from its frame.   The garden was
laid out according to the French plan—neat beds
of vegetables bordered with flowers around the
edges.

Miss Somers stooped to pick some of the
fragrant old-fashioned pinks.

"Annette, I wish you and Marie to walk with
me to Shadrach Bond's place.   My sister is
very desirous of a receipt Mrs. Bond promised
her."

"Ah, yes, thank you, Ma'm'selle. I shall be so pleased to accompany you, and also to assist Madame."

Miss Somers remained in the garden while Annette went into the house to change her gown. When she reappeared they immediately set out for Marie's, to invite her to join them.

"I never need to be persuaded, dear Ma'm'-selle. You know how willing I am to be in your company."

"Thank you, Marie."

They were soon in the cultivated fields about the Bond place.

"How Monsieur Bond loves the fox-hunting! Next fall, Annette, you will be awakened from many a morning nap by the hounds rushing over the 'commons,' barking vociferously as they pass, and Monsieur Bond hoarsely calling them after him. His friends say that he keeps a fine pack of hounds."

"His friends think he has a good *chef* also, Marie. They love to meet around his hospitable board."

"He is handsome, Annette, now isn't he?"

"You think all tall men are handsome, Marie. How is that? Is Monsieur Waring handsome too?" teased Annette.

"Oh, Annette," said Marie, looking confused.

They were near the house. It was a two-story mansion, built of brick. There were rooms on both sides of the large hall passing through the center. Handsome casings of walnut framed the door and windows. The railing and stairs were of the same wood.

Mrs. Bond's greeting was dignified. A reserved woman in plain, dark attire, but with a white gauze kerchief over the neat dress, and a white cap on her head. It was her habit to wear these accessories. A woman, however, of great kindness of heart.

Miss Somers inquired after the health of her family.

"The children are well. Shadrach is away so much. All the talk at the table is about the proposed State. The gentlemen get quite warm over it at times."

"There are some people opposed, of course?" answered Miss Somers.

"There are always a certain class who oppose every measure that comes up. It is their nature to dislike change. How is your sister, Madame Chartran, to-day?"

"As usual, thank you."

"Are the flowers doing well?"

"In excellent order."

The good ladies continued to chat upon various domestic topics. In the meantime, Minerva Humphreys, a niece of Mrs. Bond, had taken Annette and Marie for a walk about the grounds.

Then an idea came into her mind.

"Girls," she said, "come. I wish to show you something."

They followed her eagerly as she led them to a room under the roof.

"See this chest —"

"Ah! ah!"

"What do you suppose that to be?" she said, holding up a bodice of white satin.

"Short puff for sleeves," said Marie.

"Rounded neck," said Annette.

"That was Aunt Bond's wedding waist. Who would think to see her now that she ever was inside of that waist? See, here is a lisse kerchief edged with lace that goes with it."

"What is this?" said Marie, diving into the cedar chest.

"Ah, a lace cap."

"I tell you, girls," said Marie, clapping her hands, "let us dress in these costumes and go

down and call on Miss Somers and Aunt Bond
in the parlor."

Marie's eyes sparkled. "Here, Annette, you
take the wedding dress. You are the most
slender."

Marie chose a blue of a delicate shade, made
with flowing sleeves; Miss Humphreys, a stiff
brocade that rustled as she walked. Annette
arrayed herself in the satin waist, and a skirt of
soft white mousseline, made with a scant skirt;
the rounded arms were bare below the puffed
sleeves, her beautiful neck and shoulders covered
with the square of lisse, which only enhanced
their charm. She had thrown one of the lace
caps coquettishly over the waves of her dark hair.
She made a low courtesy to the girls.

"Annette, *charmante*," cried Marie. "You
do not look like yourself, or anybody else I ever
saw," she added.

"What will Madame Bond say?"

"Come," said Marie, leading the way. She
smiled mischievously at the astonishment of the
ladies, whose chat was interrupted by the entrance of the trio.

Mary and Ellen Bond, two little girls, were
in their wake, with wide-open eyes.

"Madame Bond holds a levee to-day, does she not?" said Marie demurely. She courtsied very low indeed to Madame, with a lovely grace.

"Certainly, my dear," Mrs. Bond replied. "It is a great pleasure, your presence on this occasion," falling in with the mood of the young girl. But her eyes were fixed upon Annette. In lovely confusion Annette stood. She was not sure that Madame would be pleased. She looked like a picture that had stepped out of its frame. "My dear, my dear. I hope that you may live to be as happy as I was when I wore that gown," said Mrs. Bond, a pensive look on her face.

"Thank you, Madame."

"I had forgotten mother's brocade was in that chest. You resemble her, and the likeness is striking in that costume, Minerva," said Mrs. Bond turning to her niece.

The girls paraded before a large mirror, then with another laugh they left the two ladies to continue their conversation.

Miss Somers, having obtained the receipt, summoned her charges and said they must now take leave. With many expressions of good will they parted with their kind hostess.

CHAPTER XX.

A.D. 1818.

The holiday season was over. The new year
that was to be full of events to old 'Kaskia was
at hand. Party spirit ran high in that day as
in this. While all were Republicans, and there
was not the incentive of party issue, yet the
wealth of expression and heat of temper and
argument manifested was fully as great when
considering the qualifications and characteristics
of the candidates. The older and more conservative element was led by Gov. Edwards, Pope,
Cook and others, while Shadrach Bond, Thomas
and Kane were leaders of the young men.

Elias Kane was a member of the convention
to draft the Constitution. In 'Kaskia he laid the
foundation of a future career that won admiration from all.

If space permitted, it would be deeply interesting to consider the elements that made up
this convention. Men whose names were after-

162

wards famous in the history and development of the State bent their energies and talents upon securing ends conducive to the welfare of the people.

The election of delegates was to be held on the first Monday in July, the convention on the first Monday in the August following. The Constitution was adopted by the convention, but was peculiar in this respect, that it was not submitted to a vote of the people. The articles, eight in all, were adapted to the needs of the people.

Antoine went with St. Gemme and Waring. They were in the lists supporting Bond and Thomas in general views. Antoine had just attained his majority and was duly filled with a sense of his dignity and importance as a part of the convention.

Waring was eagerly interested, for here was an opportunity to use his powers of oratory.

St. Gemme had been mixed up with the affairs of the Territory for a length of time and was really interested that the measures proposed for the new government should be wise and efficient. The Governor and Lieutenant Governor were to be elected by the people, the other officers by the Assembly.

The State government was to be established
in October.

"Ah, that is as it should be; very good," said
Monsieur Beauvais. "Monsieur Bond is prudent
and sagacious and will make a wise head. And
Pierre Menard, do we not all know that he has
been President of the Council all these years?
Did you say that now he would be the presiding
officer of the Senate? Ah, that is well, that is
just as it should be."

Monsieur Beauvais, like many others, although
opposed to any change, was entirely willing to
reap the benefit that might accrue from a new
order of things.

During the excitement of the various elections
Antoine was drawn into close contact with a
class of associates whose influence upon him was
of an objectionable nature. He was much away
from home. Annette sadly missed their old
companionship. In fact, their intimacy had not
been the same since he returned from New
Orleans. His outlook was broader now. Affairs
and men interested him more. During the fall
he and Louis spent much time in the hunt.

"Louis, you are more at home with us than
in 'Le Vieux Village.'"

"I do not wonder that you say so, Antoine, for I am here the greater part of the season. *Grandpere* Vallé complains most dolefully of my desertion. But the old house is gloomy. The *grandpere* is fond of dozing in his chair. Now what am I to do while he is engaged in that manner?"

"The young girls—they would be glad of your society," said Antoine.

"It may be," said Louis indifferently. "I know not why I am so attached to 'Kaskia, unless because it was my mother's home." To Louis this was a sacred memory. He had idolized his mother.

"I do not remember my mother. I think that if she had lived my home would have been a brighter one."

"But you are better off than I. You have your sister. Annette is good and kind to you."

"Yes," answered Antoine, feeling a twinge of regret that he had neglected Annette's claims of late.

Louis was two years older than Antoine. The scenes that 'Kaskia had passed through that fall aroused his enthusiasm. Heretofore the pleasures of life had sufficed for him. His grandfather had sent him to school two years at the

college in Maryland.　He had not been neglected
as too many of the French were.　Even those who
had been themselves educated had been careless
in regard to their children's needs.　The country
was not in a condition to favor schools.

Antoine's accomplishments were those of the
manly sports, in which he was an expert.　He
was surprised at the earnestness with which
Louis said:

"Antoine, did you read that line in the
Herald?"　He lifted his head and added with
flashing eyes:　"Some day I too will represent
the people in Congress."

"How will you go, Louis?" asked Antoine with
a laugh.　"Will you and Madame Vallé make
the long distance from here to Washington on
horseback, as did Gov. Bond and his lady?"

Louis flushed at the question.

"Which one of the reigning belles is to own
your heart, Louis?"

"That fair one is yet to appear."

"You are much too obdurate."

"The walls of my fortress will tumble all at
once, some day," said Louis, gayly, and changed
the subject.

At the end of the day their long tramp had

brought them within sight of Henry Leven's. The night was settling down in gloom.

"No stars to-night, Antoine."

They were tired. The game bags were heavily weighted. But as the light shone brighter on a nearer approach, they involuntarily quickened their steps at the thought of rest and shelter.

CHAPTER XXI.

THE FROLIC AT LEVEN'S.

THEY were not far from Henry Leven's place.
The young men, tired as they were with the
long tramp and the weight of the heavy game
bags they carried, hastened their steps as the
lights shone brighter on a nearer approach, and
the faint tones of a violin fell upon their ears.

Refreshment and shelter were at hand, but
the murmur of voices and occasional loud laughter indicated that some merrymaking was going on
within the house. When the door was thrown
open, in response to a sharp rap by Antoine, a
lively scene presented itself. Henry Leven's
daughter was standing on a stool in one corner,
her nimble fingers were chasing a familiar air
over the strings, and the flying feet of several
couples on the floor kept time to the inspiring
music. The eyes of the girl were gleaming with
fun, her cheeks a bright red, her hair disarranged
somewhat in the excitement of the moment.

"A dance at Leven's! How lucky we are, Louis," said Antoine, in an undertone, as the crowd rushed over the puncheon floor and cried in eager voices to the new-comers:

"Come in, come in."

"Ah, Antoine, you have good fortune," exclaimed a girl of sixteen, with eyes like stars and a dimple on either side of the pretty mouth as she smiled at him in her greeting.

"Yes, Louis and I have done a fair day's work. You know Louis?" he queried, glancing at his friend.

"No," replied the girl shyly, but she noted with admiration the well made figure and frank countenance of Louis. The latter almost forgot to acknowledge this unceremonious introduction.

"I'll never look farther," he thought.

Antoine turned to Louis in surprise, but just then Henry Leven strode forth from an inner room and said in a hearty voice:

"Come in, lads, come in; there is always a welcome for the traveler at my house—that you know well. Can we not find something in the way of supper for them, wife?"

While our two hunters were in Mrs. Leven's hospitable care, the young people were carrying

on the fun in a vigorous manner. The bashful-
ness apparent in the earlier part of the evening
had now worn away, and the enjoyment was at
its height.

A number were out from the village, Baptiste
and Marie among the rest. A few of the elders
were always at these gatherings to see that the
hilarity was not beyond bounds, although they
would take part with the others in the frolic.

When Antoine and Louis reappeared there
was a universal call: "Come, take partners;
we are just forming another set." No amount
of protest would excuse them.

"Antoine, you need not say that you are tired,"
pouted Marie, "for, if there was a deer in sight,
you would, with that heavy gun, follow it for
miles." And she tossed her pretty head.

"Well, cousin, just because it is you," he said,
taking her hand and leading her to the position
of head lady; then, bowing with mock deference,
he asked whether she was satisfied.

"Louis," he cried, "be our opposite."

But Louis was searching for Julie. She had
gone into another apartment and was sitting
quietly by the side of her married sister. When
he had found her, he said in a low voice: "May

I not have the pleasure of the next dance?" and his eyes looked beseechingly into hers. There were few girls that could withstand an appeal from Louis, for they liked him instinctively and were disposed to please him. Julie arose and they took their place on the floor. Baptiste and the daughter of Henry Leven were to the left of Marie, while one of the sons of the house and his fiancée formed the fourth couple.

Louis endeavored to keep up a desultory conversation in the pauses of the dance, but Julie was unusually reticent.

"What, Julie trying to be dignified?" whispered Baptiste to Marie as he passed her.

"Impossible."

"Why impossible?" he answered. "Julie is a sweet girl—"

"What says Louis just now, Baptiste? See how she smiles and blushes?"

"What does one say to a pretty girl? Some compliment, of course."

Louis was telling Julie of an incident that his grandfather had related scores of times. "Your father acted nobly on that occasion."

"Thank you, Monsieur. I have heard him say that he did only what he considered to be his duty."

"I have often thought that I should like to meet Monsieur," said Louis.

"I doubt not but that it would give him pleasure to see you at his home when he learns that your grandfather was his old Colonel," she said gravely. If she suspected anything, she did not show it by her manner.

"I shall be only too happy," he commenced, but a "Chassez allez" interrupted his sentence.

"Glances from starry eyes are deadly lances," teased Marie as she passed him in the dance.

"Nonsense," Louis replied, but he looked involuntarily in the direction of the beautiful eyes.

Julie was simply attired, but she wore her plain gown with an air that a society belle might have envied, for there was a harmony of outline in the apparent simplicity—the most difficult effect to be achieved by art.

Figure followed figure until even Marie was willing to cry "enough." A Virginia reel succeeded this set, and yet another, until Henry Leven called, "Hold there, it is time that you should rest—and count your apple seeds," he added, with a twinkle in his eyes. In his hands he bore a pan of tempting apples, which he proceeded to offer to the company. Plates piled high with Mother Leven's ginger-bread were then brought out, and pails, in which were placed gourds for dippers, for the use of those who perchance might be thirsty, and it may be that, while one contained water, the contents of others had more or less of that same *tafia* that formed part of the early cargoes.

Impromptu seats had been placed around the room. They were made of rough planks taken from the mill, and the ends supported by chairs or stools. A high fire-place was on one side, in which a few embers were burning brightly, but, fortunately for the dancers, the chimney was capacious, and swallowed up the heat given off by the blaze.

Louis and Julie were seated a little apart.

"Were is Annette to-night?"

"She cares not for these gatherings—so says Marie."

"Poor Annette is too grave for a girl of her years; it is not becoming."

"Do you not like a girl to be serious?" asked Julie, a smile lurking around the corners of her mouth.

"I do, sometimes," answered Louis with a meaning look.

Julie blushed and turned the subject by saying, "Ah, you have not named the apple."

"Yes, but I have," he replied in a gay tone.

"Then I must count the seeds." And she laid them in the palm of her hand and in a mock-serious manner concluded with:

"Eleven, he courts,
Twelve, he marries."

"Is not that a good fortune? There, it is all settled for me. Whom did you name it, Monsieur?"

"I am glad that it is settled," he answered, a wonderful light coming into his countenance, "for I named it myself. Shall we let it stand, Julie?"

She looked frightened at the intensity of his tones, and, hesitating a moment, replied: "I do not think I quite understand you, Monsieur Vallé."

"Yes, you do, Julie," he answered quietly. "What say you, Ma'm'selle?" Julie remained silent. "On your heart, Julie, you consent," he said in a low voice as he bent forward as if to pick up a forgotten core that had fallen to the floor.

It was one of those cases of which we read,

but no one believes in their actual occurrence.

"Come! on with the dance!" And the crowd arose, and there was a rush for places and shouts of laughter over unsuccessful attempts to maintain positions. Julie knew not what to think the remainder of the evening. Was Louis in earnest or not, or was their conversation merely a byplay to him? He seemed to be entirely engrossed with others and gave no further notice to her; hence she could not decide.

Marie was loth to give up the dance, but the elders announced in a very decided way that it was quite time to take leave of their kind friends. In the bustle of the departure, while adieus were being said, and refractory horses, tired with standing, must be quieted, Louis found an opportunity to whisper in Julie's ear: "I shall see you within the next fortnight," and, taking her hand in his, touched his lips to it lightly in cover of the friendly darkness.

Julie spoke no word on the homeward ride.

"What ails thee?" asked the married sister; "art weary with the tripping of the dance?"

There were tears in Julie's eyes, and had she endeavored to reply, it would surely have been in a tearful voice.

CHAPTER XXII.

SCHEMES.

"ANTOINE, papa is not so well this winter. Do you not see it?"

"I have seen that he is more infirm, and that he cares less to be out."

Annette observed him carefully. "That is all he sees. What ails Antoine these days?" So ran her thoughts, but she said: "If you meet Dr. Fisher ask him to drop in some time just as if it were a call. Papa would not listen to our consulting a physician regularly, as if it were serious."

"Why, Annette, do you think there is need of—"

"I think, Antoine, we should not be neglectful."

The Doctor called that week. Monsieur Beauvais enjoyed his cheerful conversation. He remained some time with Monsieur. Annette found occasion to speak with him alone before he left.

Dr. Fisher confirmed her suspicions, but said there was no reason for immediate alarm, unless a shock of some kind should befall him. Annette thanked the Doctor for his interest.

"I shall have his case in mind," said the Doctor, kindly. "Do not be disturbed, Annette."

"I can not help the uneasy feeling. I have had this dread for months. You will not mention this to any one?"

"Assuredly not, child." She looked relieved.

Baptiste of late had been very friendly in his overtures to Antoine. It had become a habit for a number of the young men to drop in upon Baptiste, after the store was closed to trade, and indulge their passion for play. It was in those days the fashion for all ranks to play for stakes, but the coterie about Baptiste went to extreme lengths. If Baptiste was frequently the winner he was careful that the sums were not so large as to excite their ire. Play was the curse of the age. Some of the finest characters among the pioneers had gone to ruin by yielding to this species of insanity, akin to that of the victim of strong drink. Antoine, the heir to a vast estate, was looked upon as legitimate prey. Baptiste knew of Annette's deep affection for her brother, and that the best way to reach her pride and humble it would be through Antoine. His selfish and calculating nature would not let him venture too far, but he felt secret delight when he saw Antoine being drawn into the vortex.

"There are plenty of men to lend you money," he would say when Antoine needed stakes. Monsieur Beauvais had a horror of debt, and was opposed to gaming. Antoine dared not apply to him for money.

A certain Charles Le Fevre made his appearance in the village that winter. He had no ostensible business, but possessed a good address and a careless *bonhommie*. He naturally fell in with the crowd about Baptiste, and Antoine and he grew to be on excellent terms with one another.

Louis was reading law at his home and less in 'Kaskia this year. St. Gemme was in Washington, and would be absent some months. Edgar Waring was very much engrossed in politics. He was endeavoring to make a name for himself. The time was propitious. The Assembly was in session, which brought many people to the village. Trade was active, reaching to Peoria, to Rock Island, and to the Rocky Mount-

ains in the West. Supplies must be sent along
the line of commerce. On the other hand, provisions and goods must be brought from the
East and North. Waring intended to rise with
the swell of the wave.

Antoine's intimate friends were thus engaged
in their personal interests. There was a sore
spot in his heart not yet healed. He could not
clasp hands with trouble. He must forget in
the society of the gay—something to absorb him
and make him forget.

CHAPTER XXIII.

MARIE'S WEDDING.

MADAME Dubreil had returned to 'Kaskia the previous fall. Edgar Waring lost no time in pleading his own cause. He was so far successful that Madame had consented that the wedding should take place in the spring. Marie had chosen the month of May. The time was drawing near. She had been in a great flutter over the trousseau for weeks.

"The pretty things that mamma brought from Paris will be most acceptable just now," said Marie. "I do not wish Monsieur Waring to think me behind the girls at Baltimore in appearance." (Waring had not given a thought to that view of the matter.) "Annette, would you wear the slippers at the wedding, or save them for the great ball in Le Vieux Village?" (Ste. Genevieve.)

"Wear them, by all means, at the wedding, Marie."

"But, then, the Rozier and the St. Gemme

and the Vallé families—I don't know how many
more of the *elite* are to be at the ball," urged
Marie.

"Then wear them again the next day, Marie."

Marie was very vain of her little feet, and the
new kid slippers brought from France were very
precious to her.

Madame Dubreil, just from the center of fashion, Paris, was a great authority. The bridesmaids consulted her, and other costumes to be
worn at the wedding were subjected to her approval. Every one was much interested, as
Marie's social nature and bright ways won friends
on all sides.

"Marie, had I known what was transpiring, I
could have brought the wedding gown with me."

"But, mamma, I did not exactly know myself." At which remark Madame Dubreil laughed.

The next best thing was to send to Philadel-
phia. Edgar Waring was impatient on account
of the delay. Any gown would do; why so
particular to have a certain kind?

"Ah, but I am not prepared to be a widow.
I expect to be married one time only, and I have
set my heart upon this particular kind of wedding
gown for that one time."

"This," said Waring, "is an overwhelming argument, and the claim must be admitted."

Marie said to him one day: "Are you sure that it is the little French girl that it is best for you to marry? Will your people be suited with Marie?"

"They are at such a distance that their views of the matter would not affect us," he replied. "We understand one another, do we not? That is more than can be said of Capt. Haines and his wife. He fell in love with a pretty French widow. She could not speak a word of English, nor could he speak a word of French. He was compelled to do his courting through an interpreter."

"Your French could be improved, but I understand you," she said archly.

"I am sure you do," he retorted. Then he said tenderly: "The language of love is universal, is it not, Marie?"

She looked at him with the trustful confidence of a child as he folded his arms about her and kissed her.

She whispered softly: "Ah, you know that it is."

The old bell pealed joyfully on the morning

of the 15th. For nearly a century had its silvery
tones called to early mass, to vespers, announced
the victories in batttle, vibrated to the joy in
the heart of the bride, or tolled the sad farewell
of a departed spirit.

Col. Menard, pacing the long gallery about
his house, heard the bells calling to high mass.
"God bless the little Marie to-day, the happiest
one of her life," he thought.

The small procession of friends who are to
attend them to the church has started. The
Reverend Father is waiting to perform the ceremony that will forever separate Marie from the
old life. She is dressed in white, with a long
white veil. The bridesmaids are also dressed
in white, with long veils.

It is not a grand pageant—a carriage was almost a thing unknown in this region at that date—
but the faces of the attendant friends expressed
a joyous spirit fitting the occasion. Arriving at
the Church of the Immaculate Conception, they
walk up the aisle, and kneel before the altar.
When the long ceremony of the Roman Catholic
service is ended the company returns to Marie's
home, where the wedding festivities will occupy
the rest of the day.

The promises to "dance at Marie's wedding" were faithfully kept by her numerous friends. Even Monsieur Beauvais felt well enough to attend and looked mildly jubilant. It was Rose who threw the handful of rice after the departing couple when, on the following day, the company, on horseback and on foot or in French carettes, merrily set out for "Le Vieux Village."

"S'pose there would be more luck in the old shoes, but dere some good wear yet in dese old moccasins," said Rose, and she decided not to waste them.

CHAPTER XXIV.

THE POINT OF THE BLUFFS.

It was during the latter part of August that Charles Le Fevre and Antoine rode out of the village in the direction of the "Orchard Gate." On the way they met a funeral cortege. Four women, dressed in black, attended the coffin, each holding in one hand a candle around which was a bow of black ribbon, and in the other a corner of the "immortal sheet," also black, which covered the bier.

Antoine and his companion drew aside and crossed themselves as the procession went by.

"A bad omen," muttered Antoine to himself.

After riding for some distance in silence, Le Fevre said to Antoine, not unkindly: "Do not let the matter worry you. Until arrangements have been made I shall not press you."

But Antoine was moody. "I see nothing ahead," he answered. "I dare not let my father, in his present condition, know of this thing. He has an absolute horror of debt, and debts of honor are especially obnoxious to him. He doesn't care for play."

"Your luck may change."

Antoine shook his head despondently. "Fortune has forsaken me. I have pursued her, like a weak fool, for the past few months, and yet I cannot break off abruptly."

But few remarks passed between them for the next three miles. Near the Point of the Bluffs their way separated. Antoine was to take a short cut toward Fort Chartres, which had been abandoned in 1772, and Le Fevre was to follow the trail to St. Louis.

"Here I must leave you, Monsieur. I will see you on your return." Waving his hand, Antoine disappeared among the brush. Le Fevre followed the trail for a half mile, then turned aside, and, tying his horse to a young sapling, threw his capote on the ground and rested his gun against a tree near by. The thicket was dense on all sides. He sat down on the capote and proceeded to take a scanty lunch from his pocket, consisting of a piece of corn-pone and a dried fish. "I will stop at New Design," he thought, "and then join a company of trappers

going up the river.   It would, perhaps, be safer."
His repast finished, he filled his pipe from the
pouch at his side, and as he smoked, his thoughts
dwelt on the gains of the night before.   His
eyes narrowed as he made a mental calculation
of the amount.   A sudden temptation came to
him.   Peering carefully about, but seeing no
one, "I'll risk it," he decided.   Taking from his
belt a leather wallet, he laid it down, and was
taking a handful of gold from the belt—alas, Le
Fevre, the ruling passion is strong in death!   A
shot pierces his left side, and he falls.

Louis was impatiently awaiting Antoine at the
rendezvous, which was the remaining angle of
old Fort Chartres.   The river had demolished
what had been one of the best planned and most
strongly built fortifications in the country.
Now there was left a debris of old cannon, fallen
walls, and the stone foundations of the officers'
quarters and the buildings used for magazine
stores.   Great trees had their roots inbedded in
the mass.

"What does keep Antoine?   I do not understand his delay."

"After two hours of wasted time," as Louis said

to himself, Antoine rode up to him, in haste.
His countenance was haggard and worn.   Louis
was struck by an appearance that was foreign to
Antoine.

"I am selfish," thought Louis.   "I have been
so absorbed in my own plans of late that I have
not noticed Antoine."   "Ah, Antoine," he said,
"is that you at last?   I have been waiting this
great while."

"I am late," replied young Beauvais mechan-
ically.   "What is it, Louis, that you wish with
me?"

"But, Antoine, you seem depressed.   What is
the cause?   Tell me."

"Not now," said Antoine, in the same dull
way.

Louis was full of his own affairs, so did not
ask Antoine further questions.   "Antoine, you
remember the frolic at Leven's.   I told you the
next morning of my impressions concerning Julie
Bienvenu.   Antoine, the first moment I saw her
I knew that my future wife stood before me.   I
did not reason.   I could not have explained.   I
simply knew it."

"Well, Louis?"

"I wish you to be a witness of our marriage
at St. Anne's."

Antoine repressed a loud exclamation that was about to escape his lips. "Louis," he said slowly, "have you considered what this involves?"

"I have, Antoine, and I am resolved that the sun shall set on Julie as my wife."

"I say no more."

"My grandfather, as you are aware, would disinherit and curse me should I marry against his will. He has his own plans for me. I am to go to France at once, and—but, Antoine, my own heart shall guide me in the choice of a wife."

"What is your plan?"

"I told Julie that she must consent to have the ceremony performed before I leave the country. She does not like the clandestine arrangement. I was so fortunate as to do the priest at St. Anne's a favor of such a nature that he feels under obligation to me—a deep obligation. We can rely upon him. Now, Antoine, you realize that all my prospects in life depend upon the strictest secrecy. Swear to me by all you hold most sacred that you will never divulge this scene you are about to witness, until I release you from your promise."

"I promise you on my honor as a gentleman."

"Swear it," said Louis.

"I do swear and pledge myself to the utmost secrecy."

They mounted their horses and started for the chapel. The village was deserted, but the chapel was attended by the hermit priest. Julie and her maid were at the priest's door. They had just arrived from an opposite direction. Antoine and an old French servant of the priest were the witnesses to the strange ceremony.

. Julie parted from her new-made husband as if in a dream. As Louis helped her to mount he whispered, "Julie, the Holy Mother protect you until we meet again, for we shall meet again, and under happier circumstances. Heaven will be merciful."

"Louis, my husband!" How proudly her lips pronounced the words.

He gazed at her long and earnestly, his eyes full of love and confidence. Louis Vallé had a beautiful nature, true to the heart's core. "Julie, if the time comes when you have need of help, call on Antoine. He is devoted to me. He is kind and unselfish." He took her hands in his and pressed them to his forehead and to his lips, then turned away.

Julie forced back the tears that welled into her

eyes, and endeavored to preserve her self-control until beyond the observance of others.

Louis was under the necessity of being present at a gathering of friends invited by his grandfather to spend the last evening at home with him. As they separated, he said to Antoine: "There are some things in life gratitude for which, if put into words, is but a tame sentiment. Only deeds can express fully and completely the depth of feeling that is aroused by this act of friendship on your part. If life is spared me, I shall prove that I am indeed grateful, my friend."

Louis left his horse on this side of the river, and, taking a canoe, crossed to the other shore and hastened to "Le Vieux Village."

After Antoine had parted from his friend he turned in the direction of old 'Kaskia, which he had left early on this eventful day. The full moon cast a splendor over the scene. His thoughts were in far off Louisiana, where moons like this had shone on those delightful evenings spent in Monsieur Perrine's garden. About half way home, through some mischance, his horse was lamed. Antoine, upon examination, said: "No use; I shall have to lie out to-night."

CHAPTER XXV.

ANTOINE AWAY.

WHEN Annette learned that her brother had not returned she was uneasy. She had felt worried about Antoine for some months. He was so restless, so unlike himself. She knew not how to account for this new phase of his character. Antoine and she had changed places; he now was the moody one. Once they had been closely associated in every interest; now they seemed to be drifting apart.

"Papa will not leave his room for another hour. I will go out and ask Rose." She found Rose leisurely preparing the breakfast. "Rose, did Antoine say anything to you about spending the night away from home?" she asked.

"No, honey. I heard him tell Risden to hab all de traps ready to go over to de plantation. Mabbe he gone dere."

Annette studied Rose for several moments.

"Rose, are you happy here, working all day

THE FIRST EXECUTIVE MANSION IN ILLINOIS.

GOVERNOR BOND'S RESIDENCE.

long? Do you ever think of some other way of living?"

"La, Ma'm'selle, what ails de chile? Here I got nuf to eat, fire to keep me warm, roof over head. Dat nuf for any darky, I say." Rose stood up majestically, her ruddy turban emphasizing the words, and a long-handled frying-pan waving in the air as she answered. She was indignant, but finally set the pan in place, and raked out some coals on the stone hearth, preparatory to cooking Monsieur's breakfast.

"Never mind, Rose. I merely asked the question, that is all."

"She'd better notice de Monsieur, and know about Antoine's goings-on, dan stand dere asking questions," muttered Rose. "You might as well hab your breakfast, honey," she said, relenting, as she saw Annette gazing through the window with a sad look on her face. "No good watching the way. He'll come of hisself afore long. Come now, Ma'm'selle, de cakes is hot. You take dem to the house, and I follow wid de coffee." All of the kitchens at that day were separated from the houses.

It was late in the forenoon when Antoine appeared, leading his lamed horse. Several of the

villagers passed him. They noticed his wan
looks.

"What is the matter with Antoine?" said one.

"He looks as if in some kind of trouble," said
another.

"Trouble? A young lad like that, with a full
purse when Monsieur is laid by?"

"I don't know about that. They tell me he
is heavily in debt, and that will eat into his
patrimony. He plays rashly. It is a surprise
to every one how he risks his money."

"Strange, Monsieur Beauvais never cared for
cards."

"Ah, Antoine keeps him in the dark, you may
be sure."

"I am sorry."

"A fine young man to ruin himself at play.
How many of our villagers do that!" And the
speaker shook his head.

Antoine went on slowly, all unconscious of the
comments that were being made on his course
of life.

"Antoine, you look wretchedly tired," was his
sister's greeting. "Where have you been? We
were so worried."

"Yes, Annette. I am tired both in body and

mind," he answered wearily, ignoring her question.

"You will be better of some refreshment, but you haven't told me where you were last night."

Antoine looked at her. How long ago it seemed since her companionship was all in all to him.

"Annette," he said gently, "do not ask me. I do not wish to speak of it."

She said no more, but he knew that she was hurt.

"Very well, Antoine," she replied, in a dignified tone.

"How is papa Beauvais?" he asked.

"He had breakfast in his own room. I have not seen him yet. Antoine," she spoke hesitatingly, "papa must not know you were away. It may be as well not to refer to it."

"Yes, we would better not," he answered, as if relieved at this arrangement.

"Rose will prepare what you wish." Annette opened a door and stepped out on the walk leading to the garden. The house seemed stifling. Her heart was full of wounded feeling at Antoine's coldness and apparent lack of sympathy.

She walked up and down the path for a time,

then went after some crumbs to throw to the birds that were flying about. It soothed her to see the little creatures eagerly taking up the feast she offered them.

After swallowing a cup of coffee, Antoine went out to the stables to leave some directions with Risden about his lame steed.

"Were any of the fellows inquiring for me last evening, Risden?"

"Believe dere was, Antoine. Yes, come to t'ink, det imp Toimetre was heah, but he not want to say what fur."

"You may have the pony ready for me when I get back. I am going to the other river."

Antoine sauntered down the street; there was no need of hurrying. He wondered what excuse he could give to his friends for disappointing them. Baptiste looked at him curiously as he entered the store and seated himself on the edge of the counter.

"What luck last night?" asked Antoine.

"Judge for yourself." Baptiste pulled a handful of small coin out of his pocket.

"Oh, your side, was it?" said Antoine, carelessly.

"Yes, but that isn't what I asked. We waited for you until our patience gave out, and then sent little Toimetre to the house, but Risden said you were away."

Antoine looked annoyed. "You needn't have taken the trouble. What matter if I was not with you?"

"But you are always with us." Baptiste looked surprised. ("Antoine is too good game to be spared easily," he thought to himself.) "Antoine, you are not grieving over your losses to Le Fevre?" said Baptiste. Antoine did not immediately reply. "You do look rather haggard," noticing Antoine more closely. "That is nothing. Your friends will accommodate you."

"I have borrowed all that I shall. Already have I worn out their patience," said Antoine vehemently.

Baptiste only shrugged his shoulders. Was he not Annette's brother, and was not he, Baptiste, only biding his time to strike most effectively?

In the meantime a number of their companions had come in to learn of any bit of news. Antoine was not in the mood for their small talk, but Baptiste was full of nonsense, and he was on the top wave of popularity with the crowd.

Antoine soon took his departure. As he entered his home, he met Annette in the hall.

"Papa wishes to see you," she said.

"Where is he?"

"In his own room," she answered.

Antoine would have avoided this interview,
but Monsieur Beauvais had brought up his
children to respect his wishes, and it was a habit
of the household to comply with his requests.
Monsieur Beauvais was peevish that day, and he
gave Antoine a round lecture upon spending his
time in idleness.

"Here am I, too feeble to go around, and
there is much that needs attention at the plantation."

"I am just going there," said Antoine, glad
to escape.

On the way the words of a letter received a
few days before burned into his brain. They
repeated themselves over and over to him:

NEW ORLEANS, Rue de la Royale.

"ANTOINE:—

"I send this message to post by my faithful Adele. Matters
are far worse with us. My heart fails me. Though my uncle
is kind, and if he could I know would avert this step, yet I
understand that he means that I shall marry the Senor de
Gonsalvo. Antoine, what shall I do? I cannot be the wife of

the Senor. I will not, I say to myself a hundred times a day, and my eyes fill with tears when I think of the brief happiness of thy presence. My uncle's pride in his business standing will cause him to sacrifice me. He is entangled with the Senor; the latter could ruin him to-morrow, if he chose. Canst thou not devise a means of rescue for thy poor

"LEONIE."

"Curses upon him!" And Antoine clutched his fist at an imaginary foe. "Could luck be harder? A thousand miles away from the one I love, my father threatened with death, and I head over heels in debt."

He was revolving various schemes in his mind when Henri met him.

"I was just wishing for you, Antoine."

CHAPTER XXVI.

A WARRANT.

Two days after the events narrated in the last chapter, the village was thrown into great excitement as the report circulated that the dead body of Le Fevre had been found in the brush. Two men had been prospecting with a view to settlement. Their dogs had acted strangely, then, barking vociferously, had disappeared in the tangle of undergrowth in the timber. The men had followed to see what had aroused the dogs. Then the remains had been discovered.

Baptiste, who was always foremost in any stir, thought at once: "I see in this my opportunity."

The news was in every one's mouth. The native French were peaceable and lived in harmony and without strife, but of late pioneers of all classes were entering the new State. A sense of outraged justice was felt spontaneously, and there was talk of law and of bringing the guilty one to punishment. In such times of fever heat,

suspicions gather, and almost any one, upon a
slight pretext, will be accused of complicity.
There was one incident that occurred at the
inquest.

"Why, that is Antoine Beauvais' knife. It
has a peculiar handle," said Baptiste in feigned
astonishment.

"So it is," said a bystander. "I've seen him
with it a dozen times."

"Yes," said Antoine, "where did you find it?"
Then he saw, with a shudder, that there were
blood-stains upon it. "I lent the knife to Le
Fevre just as we parted at the 'Point of the
Bluffs.'" He reached out his hand for the knife.

"No," said the Sheriff, "it was found near the
body. We will keep that for the present."

"In which direction did you go then?" asked
a neighbor of Antoine in low tones. "Did you
see any one prowling about?"

"No," said Antoine, answering only the last
question. He then turned away. He did not
wish attention called to the direction he had
taken.

It was supposed that the Rangers had cleared
the country of unfriendly Indians. No reports
of hostile bands at this time were heard. It was

known that Le Fevre was rather careless, and
that he carried large sums of money with him.
But who was the murderer?

Antoine spent the evening in writing to Leonie.
He told her that her letter was in his thoughts
day and night.

"Alas, and had I wings that I might fly to your relief! But
you are hundreds of miles away, and are to be made a sacrifice
while I am held here powerless to aid you. My father is suffering with a malady of a strange character, and he must not be
excited in any way. The chief care of dear Annette is to guard
him from all worry or alarm. I am in a sad case—my duty to
him—yet when I think of my Leonie, and her equally great need,
I am wild. Entreat the *tante* to delay by every means in her
power the dread consummation of this affair. If the worst
comes, Leonie, take the faithful Adele and fly to the convent.
The good sisters, with whom you are such a favorite, will surely
shelter you. Ask them for their protection, until you see or hear
further from your devoted

"ANTOINE.

"P. S. A strange murder has been committed not far from
the village. Charles Le Fevre was the victim.

"A. BEAUVAIS."

He sealed and addressed the letter in his stiff
chirography to "Mlle. Leonie de Villiers, Rue
de la Royale, Nouvelle Orleans, Louisiana,"
and delivered the missive into the hands of the
carrier to Vincennes who started the next day
on his rounds.

The talk of the Le Fevre murder was gaining ground. A suspicious atmosphere was gathering about Antoine Beauvais. Some there were who said that he could tell more about it if he chose. His troubled countenance was commented on. He certainly was unlike himself.

How does a storm gather? The scattered and flying clouds unite in one great outburst of overwhelming disaster!

The day arrived when two constables rode up to the Beauvais premises and asked Risden, who was working about the stable door, if Antoine Beauvais were at home.

"Oui," he answered.

"Show us to him."

The frightened darky led the way.

"Bad business this," muttered the constable under his breath. "I'd 'most rather be shot myself than have to serve this warrant on old Monsieur Beauvais' son."

As Risden turned the corner, they found Antoine training his favorite horse.

"Antoine Beauvais," the constable commenced in his court tone of voice, and read the warrant.

Antoine became deathly white during the reading. In a flash he saw it all—the strange and averted looks of his companions, their hushed conversation at his approach.

"Ah, *mon Dieu*, my promise to Louis!"

"Constable," he said in a voice strange to his own ears, "I am not guilty—no one could believe that."

"If that is the case, all you need do is to prove an alibi." Antoine looked at him blankly. "I must take you with me. I am very sorry, but the law summons you."

"You need not apologize. I did not realize that that must follow," Antoine said in a strained voice. "My father must not know. *Mon Dieu*, it will kill him!" He buried his face in his hands and groaned aloud. "I must see Annette," he added, striving to regain his self-control. "Risden, find Ma'm'selle Beauvais."

Risden's usually loquacious tongue was quiet. He brought Annette to her brother. Antoine threw his arms around her.

"Annette," he said, "I have sad and grievous news for you. Can you bear—"

"What is it, Antoine?" she asked in alarm.

"Annette, I am under arrest for the murder of Le Fevre."

"You, Antoine? There is some terrible mistake," she exclaimed, as she clung to him. She looked around at the men as if to ask, "Why are you here?"

"Le Fevre was murdered on the 17th of August."

She started. That was the night that—

She raised her head from Antoine's shoulder and looked into his eyes, as if to read his very soul.

A sickening sense of suffocation came over him. He saw the thought that was in her mind.

"Annette, I understand you, but matters will be righted. I cannot explain just now, but time will unravel the complication." He hesitated; then added: "Papa is on your hands, Annette."

As he said this Annette's young form took on an additional dignity. Her face, though pale with emotion, was even haughty as she looked at the constable.

"He must not know," she said. "I understand, quite, Antoine."

CHAPTER XXVII.

ANNETTE waited in vain for Antoine, but Risden kept his own counsel. The neighbors did not call that day. People did not feel free in Monsieur Beauvais' presence; there was that fine reserve about him which keeps back familiarity. Waring was engaged in the preliminary proceedings, and St. Gemme was at "Pain Court." On Monsieur Beauvais' account Waring would not let Marie go to the house. He feared that she might be indiscreet in her remarks. "Wait till we know something of the result," he said.

Monsieur Beauvais was in a restless condition all day, and Annette was in constant attendance upon him. As evening approached she called Risden.

"Why does Antoine stay so long, Risden?"

"Don't you know, honey?"

"No, what is it, Risden?"

"If dey should put him in—"

"In what?"

"Dat is, I t'ink he will stay with some of them to-night," Risden stammered.

Risden had slipped off and hung about the trial, wishing to keep track of his young master. He felt as if he could have knocked down the whole set of rascals who were trying to harm Antoine. He caught a glimpse of Baptiste's face once through the crowd. An exultant gleam crossed it at some unfavorable turn to Antoine.

The old French of high standing were shaking their heads and talking excitedly. Beauvais *fils*—preposterous! One of the oldest families. It was all the fault of the new government. Any one of them might now be interfered with and molested. They had gotten along for a hundred years with very little law; now they had too much, entirely too much.

Annette was weighed down with a feeling of utter helplessness. "What must I do?" she asked herself over and over again. "If only Monsieur St. Gemme were here. What if papa should ask for Antoine?"

Monsieur Beauvais was dozing in a chair in his room.

"Papa, are you ready for your tea?"

"Is that you, Annette?   What did you wish?"

"I thought you might have tea now."

"Yes," he replied absently.

Rose presently brought the tray, and Annette arranged all to her father's satisfaction.   Monsieur was more flighty than usual to-night, due perhaps to the disturbance of the elements.

Annette was full of impatience, but restrained it before the Monsieur.   Her pale face had a drawn look upon it, at variance with her years. As she heard the sound of the wind rushing along the river, "I feel as if I were being drawn out into fine wire," she exclaimed. Every nerve was quivering.   She arose to close a swinging blind.   A thought came to her: "I must see Col. Menard to night and ask his advice.   I must speak with him."   Poor Annette, it was not easy for her to speak of family matters.

She sought Risden again.

"Risden, was Col. Menard over the river to-day?"

"I t'ink not, Ma'm'selle.   I heard some of de darkies saying dat some of the Colonel's big re-lations down from St. Louis—I t'ink Monsieur Choteau himself, and some of de Gratiots. Dey have big times over to de place."

THE MENARD MANSION, KASKASKIA, ILLINOIS.

This was unexpected, but she held to her plan.

"Risden, watch; if papa calls, say that I am out for a little while."

"Ma'm'selle Annette, I t'ink a storm is coming on."

The wind whistled about the buildings.

"That will do," said Annette, with dignity. "Do not let Rose know."

The dusk was at hand; she must hasten. Throwing on a large wrap that completely enveloped her, and letting the hood fall over her face, she hurriedly took a short cut to the river. On the bank lived young Charle Danis and his aunt. The latter was very deaf.

"If Charle should be away—" she thought, but he opened the door in answer to her tap.

"Charle," said Annette in a low voice, "come outside."

"Ma'm'selle Beauvais!" he exclaimed in astonishment.

"Hush, and come with me," said the girl.

He shut the door and stepped out into the gathering dusk.

Annette said hurriedly: "I wish you to get the canoe and take me over the river. I must see Col. Menard."

"It can not be.   The storm is coming."

"It must be."

The young ferryman would not be outdone by a girl in courage.   "Is it about Antoine?"

"Yes," she said briefly.

"One moment."

He came out with the oars and led the way down to the river.   The thunder was muttering in the distance.   The flashes of lightning showed their course.   The waves were rising before the wind, and lines of white foam on the shore were revealed by the incessant flashes.

They were soon on the other side, and Danis helped Annette up the steep bank, first taking the precaution to draw his light boat far up on the sands.   He was, like all the French youth, naturally gallant, and the trouble he knew Annette to be in called out his sympathy, but respect for her kept him silent.

"Charle," said Annette, as they came in sight of the brilliantly lighted mansion, "there are guests here from above, and I must avoid seeing them.   We will go around to the back entrance."

Skirting the spring-house, they ascended a little rise in the ground and stole along in the shadow of the house.

Annette whispered: "Knock at the door and ask for Monsieur le Colonel. Go quickly." She shrank back in the corner.

It so happened that Col. Menard opened the door of the dining-room and stepped out to view the coming storm.

"Monsieur," said the lad.

"Who is it—Danis?"

"Yes, and young Ma'm'selle Beauvais is with me. She wishes to see you about Antoine."

The wind blew out the lighted candle in the room. Col. Menard stepped outside upon the stone flags and closed the door behind him.

"*Mon Dieu*, and such a night! Ask her in," said the Colonel in kindly anxiety.

They were standing in a covered passage paved with large flag-stones. This passage led to the kitchen. Annette, hearing their voices, and recognizing Col. Menard's, came forward.

"Ah, my child, dear child, come with me." He led her to the end of the passage, opened the door, and drew her forward before the glowing coals in the capacious chimney. "Here, you must warm; you are chill with the night air, my child. The house is full of guests, but here we are alone, for Elise has gone to gossip with her people in one of the cabins; she will not return in an hour. Here we may talk undisturbed. Tell me everything. A great risk for you, my child, a very great risk."

"Col. Menard, my papa and Antoine—" she said, brokenly.

Col. Menard listened with ready sympathy.

This trait in his character, which enabled him to enter into the joys and sorrows of others, made him universally beloved.

"It will kill him," Annette continued. "This terrible accusation! How could they charge Antoine with this crime, and he so gentle and kind to every one?" She was trembling violently.

"I know, my child. I did not think that they would carry this so far. His refusal to account for himself on that day is going against him."

"I do not understand that myself. Antoine has been sad for some time. We have much trouble, Monsieur."

"Yes, I understand that Monsieur Beauvais' health is failing."

"It is not that alone, Monsieur," she faltered. "It is not known, but it is papa's mind." And here she sobbed in great agony and distress. It hurt her pride to say the words. "That has been giving way—and the result of this—of this—"

A great clap of thunder crashed over them and reverberated with sharp intonation. about the cliffs at their back. The place was a glare of light. Annette gave a half shriek. Her nerves were unstrung, and it seemed as if the end of all things was at hand.

Col. Menard put his hand reassuringly upon her head. "There, you are safe, child, but you must not think of returning home to-night."

"Ah, but, Monsieur, I must—I could not leave papa alone. I am away too long as it is. Monsieur, how shall I break the sad news to him?" she asked, piteously.

"You must not. He must be kept in ignorance of all until the trial is over. There is no doubt but Antoine will be cleared. We must get for him the best counsel that can be found. I will see you in the morning. I will call and inquire after Monsieur Beauvais' health, and then we will see."

The rain was now coming down in torrents, amid vivid flashes of lightning and roars of thunder. Young Danis pushed open the door and asked to enter.

"Come in, Danis; we are thoughtless to leave you in this weather."

"No matter, Monsieur; the rain has just commenced. I think it will soon be over."

Annette lapsed into silence. She would rest upon the judgment and advice of Monsieur Menard. The Colonel saw that she was ignorant of the real feeling of the villagers as to the murder, but thought it best not to inform her.

The falling drops now came splashing down the large chimney. The lightning illumined the gray walls and the wide hearth. A high mantel shelf was fastened across the chimney. It had either been painted black, or had darkened with age and the fumes arising from cooking. An immense crane on one side was firmly imbedded in the rock of the chimney. A long-handled spit stood at one side. An opening to the right of the flue led into the oven that was built round about the chimney on the outside. Many had been the banquets given by Col. Menard to his numerous friends, and the baking and brewing for the great feasts had been brought to perfection in this old rock kitchen.

"Ma'm'selle," said Col. Menard as the storm abated, "you must have some refreshment before you return." He went into the house, and, taking some wine from the sideboard that stood in the hall, he brought it to her. "Here, drink that," he insisted. "I shall see you as far as the river." Although Annette protested, Col. Menard's courtesy would not allow him to leave anything undone for the young Ma'm'selle.

The clouds had broken; the stars were appearing here and there through the rifts, and a new moon was showing in the western horizon when Col. Menard placed his charge carefully in the frail boat.

"Charle, see that Ma'm'selle Beauvais reaches her home in safety."

"That I will, Monsieur; you may depend on me."

"I know it, lad."

"Adieu, Monsieur," said Ma'm'selle, "I am deeply grateful for your kindness."

"Do not mention it, Ma'm'selle."

Danis pulled rapidly across the dark water. As he left Annette at her home he said:

"If Ma'm'selle has need of Charle Danis she will call upon him."

"Thank you, yes." And she disappeared within the door.

CHAPTER XXVIII.

A MATTER OF INQUIRY.

ANNETTE was permitted to visit Antoine at certain intervals.

"Annette, do not ask me," he said in one of their talks; "it distresses both of us—I cannot answer you."

"But, Antoine, they say: 'If he is innocent, why does he not state where he was and so end it?'"

Antoine looked at her, and in his eyes was the expression of the hunted deer.

"Annette, that I am innocent God knows. It cannot be otherwise but that I will be cleared."

"But papa—Antoine, how can you be obdurate when you think of him?"

A spasm of pain contracted his features.

"Papa does not know—" He hesitated.

"I have kept all from him, but I know not how much longer I may be able to do so."

"Has any word come from Louis?" asked Antoine irrelevantly. He had written a letter telling Louis of his situation, but weeks or months would elapse before he could hope for a reply.

Annette left him, wondering at his course.

Col. Menard had secured the ablest counsel in Antoine's defense. Waring was to assist. Menard called frequently at the Beauvais' home, to engage Monsieur in conversation upon various topics.

"You must have rest, Ma'm'selle," he would say to Annette. "I will sit with the Monsieur the next hour."

Col. Menard found Monsieur Beauvais under the impression that Antoine had gone off on a trading expedition. He asked regularly, "Will Antoine come to-day or to-morrow?" Risden could have explained had he chosen; for the night that Annette had gone, over to Col. Menard's Monsieur Beauvais had asked for Antoine. Risden knew not exactly what to answer.

"Ah, Monsieur, Antoine—he gone away with some men." This answer had lingered in Monsieur Beauvais' mind, although he replied: "Too soon to hunt, Risden, if it is for game."

"I t'ink it was some kind of game dese men wanted," said Risden solemnly.

Monsieur St. Gemme had concluded his business and returned home. He had heard on the way a garbled account of Antoine's misfortune, and went immediately to Waring's office.

"What is all this trumpery about? Tell me."

Waring gave him a detailed account.

"Preposterous! Who has pushed matters to this point? A new clan are coming in, you remember."

"Well I am of the new clan," said Waring.

"You know what I mean," said St. Gemme impatiently. "A certain jealousy of the old families."

"St. Gemme, do you know I believe Baptiste Lalonde has a finger in this? I know not of a certainty, but I have been watching him."

"If he has I will call him out," said St. Gemme hastily.

"Don't spoil our plans with your impatience. These are only impressions, but if they prove to be true, I'll help you out with it." And Waring's honest blue eyes flashed with indignation.

"Josephine," said St. Gemme, after he had refreshed himself, "I am going over to Monsieur Beauvais'."

"Do; I am sure they need your assistance just now. I have been there a number of times while you were away. Annette is a walking ghost. I believe that Monsieur does not receive visitors."

"I shall inquire at any rate."

In truth he was tired with several days' hard riding, but he forgot all in his anxiety for the Beauvais family. "Two years ago one of the most peaceful households in the village, and now—"

St. Gemme entered the gate and walked to the house. Annette herself opened the door for him.

"*Je suis enchantee,*" she exclaimed in her joy at his return.

"I arrived to-day, and you, Annette?" he said as he entered the large reception hall.

"You have heard?" she said faintly.

"Yes, everything. Annette, what is this about Antoine's strange persistence?"

"I do not know. I cannot, cannot understand it. Father does not understand, Monsieur St. Gemme." She lifted her fine eyes to his. "You have noticed in my father—?" She stopped, as if she couldn't frame the words.

"I know, Annette," he said with ready tact.

"Was that what you meant when you talked with me at the old mill?"

"That was it. I had seen your father in an attack that I felt was a warning. He requested me not to mention it, as he did not want his children to be alarmed."

"Papa is resting in the belief that Antoine is with the *couriers du bois*. We do not admit visitors into his presence, and in fact few come these days."

St. Gemme looked angry. He did not know whether it was delicacy or suspicion that kept them away. He was afraid that it was the latter.

"He will see you," continued Annette. "I desire that you should see him."

"Thank you. I came for that purpose. Annette, there is something of which I wish to speak to you, but do not answer unless you wish."

She looked at him in surprise.

Monsieur St. Gemme would not acknowledge to himself that this girl, with her intense nature, possessed for him a fascination that he could not explain. It pained him to see how thin the contour of her face had become. He hardly knew how to put his question. He did not wish to inquire into her personal affairs, but Waring's remarks in regard to Baptiste had suggested an idea to him.

"Did Baptiste Lalonde have any thought of asking your hand in marriage, Annette? Pardon me, but certain things have led me to believe that such might be the case."

Annette appeared to be annoyed. "I would rather not mention—it is a subject which is very disagreeable to me."

St. Gemme asked no more. He had the clew to Baptiste's actions.

"I think I hear papa calling," said Annette. "Will you go to him now?"

"Yes, if you wish."

Monsieur Beauvais greeted St. Gemme with a pleased smile. His mind was clearer to-night than it had been for several days, but St. Gemme noted with sorrow the great change that had taken place.

"It has been an age since you were here. I have missed our long talks."

"I have been away," (taking the wasted hand).

"Not for pleasure?"

"No," said St. Gemme, smiling, "you could not call it pleasure. There were conflicting claims, the old French grant being overlapped by the British. What with Virginia, the two Territories and our State, the various governments have made the subject of land grants inexhaustible."

Annette left the gentlemen to a discussion of the old titles to land.

CHAPTER XXIX.

ALARM.

MONSIEUR BEAUVAIS improved for some days after St. Gemme's visit, and was able to walk about the house and grounds to some extent. Now that her mind was relieved as to her father, Annette's thoughts were constantly with Antoine. The time of his trial was drawing near. If her father could only be kept in ignorance until after that had taken place, then could they take a trip to France and forget this blight upon their house. Annette would not believe but that Antoine would be cleared.

Risden and Jule were in the stable one day, arguing the pros and cons of the situation.

"I tell you there's a poor show for Monsieur Antoine," said Jule. "It will go hard with Monsieur Beauvais if the jury—how do he stand it anyway, Risden?"

"He doan' know nuffin about it," said Risden.

"They say that Antoine play very hard and

this Monsieur Le Fevre win all that Antoine have."

"I doan' believe it.   Nebber could have done it," said Risden.

"They say, too, that Antoine quarrel very bad with Le Fevre before he—"

The two servants were startled by a moan, and then a heavy thud, as of some one falling.

They rushed out and found Monsieur Beauvais lying flat on the ground. He was faintly breathing, but unconscious.   His face was livid.

"Run, Jule, for Ma'm'selle and Rose.   I will carry Monsieur to de house," said Risden in a horror-stricken tone. Had Monsieur heard their foolish talk?   No; he was too far away!

Risden lifted Monsieur Beauvais in his strong arms to carry him to the house.

Jule tried to prepare Annette, but she knew instantly what had happened.   The physician had warned her that this might be the end.

"Bring papa into his room, Risden," she said in an unnaturally calm voice.   "Jule, run for Monsieur St. Gemme and the physician." Others coming in to help, Annette left her father to their care and went into the hall and sat down in a dazed way.

"Annette is stunned," they whispered. They came and went all day. Dr. Fisher could give them no hope. Monsieur Beauvais might live for some weeks, even months in this condition.

Col. Menard called to express his sympathy and grief at the heavy blow that had fallen upon the Beauvais household.

"Ma'm'selle, poor child, I feel for you," he said as he clasped Annette's hand at parting.

"I know, Monsieur." Her eyes were heavy with grief.

Menard's noble heart was full of kindness and sympathy for others, and he was touched as she turned upon him her great eyes with their look of deep sadness.

It was St. Gemme who told Antoine.

"I alone am to blame. I am the cause of all this woe," Antoine cried in desperation. "Annette, you are suffering for my wrong-doing." He groaned aloud.

Monsieur St. Gemme, who did think Antoine much to blame for the course he had pursued, nevertheless tried to comfort him in regard to his father by stating that Monsieur Beauvais was in ignorance of Antoine's situation.

"Thank Heaven for that."

"Perhaps it would be as well to thank Annette's watchful care," said St. Gemme dryly.
"When will you make up your mind to break
this unseemly silence—unless there is a cause
for it?" he added meaningly.

Antoine looked at him reproachfully.

"St. Gemme, I am not—" Then he broke
off abruptly. Monsieur waited, but as Antoine
said no more he left without other questioning.

That evening St. Gemme made another call
at the Beauvais home to see if anything further
was needed for the night. Annette was with
her father. She fancied that he had some
knowledge of her presence, and had spoken to
him, hoping to obtain some sign of recognition,
but in vain.

"Risden, you remain with papa and call me if
he stirs," said Annette, as she heard Monsieur
St. Gemme's voice in the hall. As she opened
the door and was about to take a few steps forward Monsieur St. Gemme noticed her extreme
pallor.

"How is Monsieur Beauvais?" he asked
quickly.

"Papa is lying quietly, but—" She reeled, and,
throwing up her hands, would have fallen to the

floor, but St. Gemme, springing forward, caught her in his arms.

He lifted her tenderly to the settee that was drawn before the chimney place, and, bringing some spirits, forced a few drops between her teeth, and then commenced to chafe her hands.

She opened her eyes and saw him kneeling at her side. "Where am I?" she asked. Then, as consciousness returned, she attempted to raise her head. "What has happened? I feel so strangely. What is it?" she asked in terror.

Monsieur St. Gemme replied to her soothingly, as he held both of her hands tightly clasped in his:

"Do not be alarmed, Annette. Your over-wrought system has rebelled for the moment. You are better now?"

"I think so," she said faintly.

He brought her a glass of wine. "Drink this."

She shook her head.

Then he said, "Rest a little while, and you will feel quite yourself again."

She closed her eyes a few minutes; her hand was still lying in his; a sense of weariness and depression was upon her; she felt herself receding and advancing as a boat upon the tide. If she were to let go of that strong grasp, she would sink down through the floor, into an infinite abyss.

"Annette, you must take something to arouse you," said St. Gemme, seeing that she did not rally from the effect of the swoon.   She obeyed him listlessly.

He was rewarded by seeing a delicate flush begin to appear in her countenance as the stimulant acted upon her system.

"Monsieur St. Gemme," she said after a long silence, "this is a bitter world, bitter indeed.   I seem doomed to have trouble as my life portion. I have never been very happy as other girls have been.   I brought sorrow at my birth, and it has ever haunted me."

"Annette, do not talk in that way.   You are young, your life is before you.   There yet may be—" He paused.   There was coming over him a great yearning to take this young creature in his arms, press her closely to his heart and shield her from all care or sorrow.   He rose abruptly and walked the length of the hall.   How was his life entangled!   As a flash it was revealed to him where he stood, but with a quick gesture of repeal, "Shall I be a coward," he asked himself, "and false to life's obligations on either hand?"

"Annette," he said very gently, as he returned to her, "because you have been true to your higher ideals of what may be required of you, the joys and sorrows of life will be at your feet. You will rise superior to life's casualties. One of the old poets has said: 'The way to conquer misfortune is to bear it.'" He raised her hand to his lips. "I will leave you now," he said in the same gentle tones, "but first I will call Rose."

Rose was crooning to herself over the kitchen fire. "The world is coming to an end—coming to an end," she repeated, rocking back and forth, and wringing her black hands.

"Rose," said St. Gemme, "Ma'm'selle has had a faint turn. Give her a hot drink as you put her to bed. She is on the verge of an illness if I mistake not." He passed out into the night.

"Rose," said Annette, "I feel as if the world were slipping away from me."

"Doan' say that, honey. It am a black night when the stars doan' shine."

CHAPTER XXX.

THE TRIAL.

THE day of Antoine's trial finally arrived.
The folio sheet published in that day made the
most of the circumstances, and reported the case
in the following manner:

"STATE OF ILLINOIS VS. ANTOINE BEAUVAIS *fils*.

"The body of Charles Le Fevre having been
found in the bush not far from the trail northwardly to St. Louis, by two men coming out of
the Okaw bottoms, great excitement prevails in
the village. By reason of various circumstances
that have come to light in connection with our
neighbor Antoine Beauvais *fils*, suspicion gathered force until it became so strong that Justice
Langeois was applied to for a warrant for Beauvais' arrest.

"A warrant was issued and placed in the hands
of the constable, who brought Beauvais before
Justices Langeois and Dumont for examination.
The evidence was considered sufficient to hold

him for trial at the next term of court, when he
was brought before the grand jury, who, after
investigation, indicted Antoine Beauvais *fils*.
The prisoner was brought into court, and, under
the advice of his attorney, pleaded, 'not guilty.'
The attorneys having signified their readiness
for the trial, it was begun. A jury was called
and sworn. The State's Attorney opened the
case by stating what he expected to prove:

"'Gentlemen of the jury, this is a somewhat
peculiar case, and we will have to rely princi-
pally upon circumstantial evidence to establish
the prisoner's guilt. In almost all cases of
murder the crime is committed under the cover
of darkness, or not under public gaze, and every
precaution is taken by the criminal to conceal it.
So in this case the crime was committed in a
lonely spot in the thicket. It will be proven
that Charles Le Fevre staid in Kaskaskia for
some time; that he left the village for the purpose, as he said, of going to St. Louis, on the
17th day of August; that his dead body was
found by two men returning from the bottom of
the Okaw River, lying in the thicket, not a
great distance from the Point of the Bluffs, on
the 20th day of August; that the prisoner was

seen about noon on the 17th of August with Le
Fevre, on the trail leading to St. Louis; that
the prisoner's knife was found near the body;
that the crime had evidently been committed
for the purpose of robbery; that the man killed
had no quarrel with any one in the village, but,
on the contrary, was on the most friendly terms
with all, was popular, a general favorite. It
will also be proven that the prsioner was much
in the company of, and had lost a large amount
of money to, Le Fevre, while playing cards with
him; that the prisoner was absent from town at
that time and utterly refused to give an account
of himself while absent. Taking all these facts
into consideration, they point strongly to the
prisoner as guilty of the crime. You will hear
the evidence and observe the manner of the
witnesses, and after giving it your careful consideration, I have all confidence that you will do
justice in the case.'

"The witnesses were then called and sworn.
The attorney for the defense, having stated that
this was a case of the last importance to his
client, his liberty, possibly his life at stake,
asked that the witnesses be separated, and those
not being examined sent out of hearing of the

trial. 'Not that I fear the conviction of my client of the crime with which he is charged, but that their testimony may not be biased before they are called upon for examination.' The court granted the request of the attorney, and ordered all witnesses sworn in the case to retire from the room, except the one called to testify.

"Mr. Hugh Maxwell was asked by the Prosecuting Attorney to state where he resided. He said that he had lived in Kaskaskia for many years.

"Prosecuting Attorney: 'This is a suit of the people of the State of Illinois for the trial of Antoine Beauvais *fils*, who has been indicted by the grand jury for the murder of Charles Le Fevre. State whether you know the prisoner, and if so, how long have you known him?'

"Mr. Maxwell: 'I have known him from a child. He was reared here.'

"Prosecuting Attorney: 'Did you know Charles Le Fevre, and what do you know of him?'

"Mr. Maxwell: 'I did, but for a short time only. He appeared to be a pleasant man, joining with the young men in their amusements, playing cards mostly.'

"Prosecuting Attorney: 'Did he play for

money, or win much money, especially from the prisoner?'

"Mr. Maxwell: 'He did, and I think he won a great deal from the prisoner; in fact, I know he did. They were much together, and appeared to be great friends.'

"Prosecuting Attorney: 'Did you know when Le Fevre left here, and was the prisoner with him then?'

"Mr. Maxwell: 'I was at the tavern when Charles Le Fevre left; the prisoner was not with him then, but it was said that the prisoner left the village at the same time.'

"Prosecuting Attorney: 'State what you know about the finding of the body.'

"Mr. Maxwell: 'Two men coming out of the bottom of the Kaskaskia River, near the Point of the Bluffs, on the trail leading to St. Louis, found the body in a thicket. They at once notified the coroner, who with his jury held an inquest, and upon investigation they were convinced that the man had been waylaid and shot by some one concealed in the bush. Evidently the body had been robbed of all valuables.'

"Prosecuting Attorney: 'Was anything found that would lead to the prisoner's committing the crime?'

"Mr. Maxwell: 'There was nothing except a knife that was said to have belonged to Antoine Beauvais.'

"No questions were asked by the defense.

"Dr. William Reynolds was next called.

"Prosecuting Attorney: 'State what you know of the condition of the body when you examined it. I am told that you were called at the inquest.'

"Dr. Reynolds: 'I was called at the inquest, and upon examination found the man had been killed by a gunshot wound, and by the direction and position of the wound, the shot must have been fired by some one concealed in the bush.'

"Attorney for defendant: 'What do you know of the prisoner?'

"Dr. Reynolds: 'The prisoner is of an amiable disposition, not given to quarrels or disputes. His family are French people, kind, always ready to assist their neighbors.'

"Michael Antay was called.

"Prosecuting Attorney: 'State whether you were one of the parties who found the body of the murdered man, and the circumstances of the finding.'

"Witness: 'It was on the 20th day of August.

Ambrose Levasseur and myself were in the Okaw bottoms, and when coming out toward the trail our dogs began to bark furiously. We went to see what they were barking at. We found the body of the dead man in the thicket. He must have been dragged. Near the body we picked up a knife which we gave to the coroner.'

"A knife was shown the witness, and he was asked if this was the knife. He said it was.

"Ambrose Levasseur corroborated the testimony of Michael Antay.

"Louis La Chapelle testified that he had known the murdered man; that he was friendly and spent much time in play; that the prisoner had lost much money to him; that the prisoner was away from town and no one seemed to know where he was on the 17th of August.

"Jean Etienne Lafont testified that he had seen the prisoner in company with the murdered man, near noon, a short distance this side of the Point of the Bluffs, on the 17th of August.

"Willaim Morrison testified that he had sold the knife to the prisoner the previous winter. He also identified the knife.

"This concluded the testimony of the State.

"The defense introduced the following:

"Pierre Menard had known the prisoner from a young lad. 'He was of an invariably kind and gentle disposition. I have never heard of any quarrel or of any difficulty with his companions, and with my intimate knowledge of his disposition and character I cannot believe him to be guilty of the crime with which he is charged.'

Gen. Edgar, William Rector, Jean Baptiste Montreville and others gave equally strong testimony as to the character of the prisoner, and none of them could believe him guilty.

"The case was closed, and the attorneys proceeded to address the jury. The attorney for the State waived the opening, and the attorney for the defense said:

"'Gentlemen, you have carefully and patiently listened to the evidence presented by the State, and you will agree with me that the prosecution have signally failed to produce any evidence whatever that my client is guilty of the crime with which he is charged. We will examine the testimony together and try to find the correct and just bearing it has upon the case, and arrive at an intelligent and just conclusion as to his guilt or innocence. If I do not repeat correctly the evidence and give it a fair construction, you

will at once detect it, and disregard all that you
find to be wrong.   You will arrive at your own
conclusion in making your verdict on the case.

"'In the first place, Mr. Maxwell, well ac-
quainted with the parties materially connected
with the case, states that the murdered man
was staying in the village for some time before
the dead body was found; that he was a gentleman of leisure, who spent most of his time in
play, and that he was a general favorite; that he
won some money, and possibly some from my
client among the rest, but that the existing re-
lations were pleasant; that my client and the
murdered man left the village on the 17th day
of August, going northwardly.   The further fact
that a knife found near the body belonged to my
client was testified to, and that Mr. William
Morrison had sold this same knife to my client,
and that my client and the murdered man were
seen by Jean Etienne Lafont, about noon of the
same day, the 17th of August, on which the
victim left for St. Louis.   We have also the
testimony of the doctor who examined the body
at the inquest, as to the manner of death.   Now,
this is the substance of the evidence that has
been presented to you, and with which they
expect to convict my client.

"'Undoubtedly the State's Attorney will dwell upon these points, and rely upon them to gain your verdict of conviction. The facts may be sufficient to direct suspicion to him, but does their fair and just application to the case, which you on your oath are bound to give, justify you in convicting him of the crime of murder, the penalty for which is death on the gallows? These facts may be the exact truth, and yet he be innocent of the crime. It is true that he lost some money to Le Fevre, but the most kindly feelings existed between them. As to his refusal to account for his absence from the village, and upon which so much stress is laid, there are various ways of explaining this absence. That he was away on business for others which he is not at liberty to disclose, and as you, or I, or any other true man would have done had we undertaken particular business for a friend, or any one, that was not to be made public—this would account for his absence.

"'As to the knife found, he does not deny that it was his, but says that he had loaned it to Charles Le Fevre. Now take the testimony of our leading citizens of the true character of the prisoner. They have known him from childhood, and have seen him almost every day of his life. The good deeds of a man are remembered and discussed a short time, but if suspicion once attacks a man, an evil tale to blacken a man's character gathers until the most incredible statements are given credence, and it often happens that when proof of a crime rests entirely upon circumstantial evidence a truly innocent person has to suffer the penalty attached to the crime by the law. Although the fate of my client depends upon your decision, I am satisfied that after consultation among yourselves you will agree with me that there is not sufficient evidence to convict, and that all these attendant circumstances can be accounted for in many ways with just force and reason. I am further satisfied that you will unanimously acquit him, and that in time the entire innocence of my client will be established and the guilty party discovered.'

"The State's Attorney in reply said:

"'Gentlemen of the jury, I must give my brother attorney credit for having in his statement to you of the testimony, and in the summing up and argument upon it, placed it in a very plausible and ingenious light in behalf of his client. But, gentlemen, there are usually two sides to all questions. That a great crime has been committed, a vicious and brutal murder of one of the people, is an evident fact. Now, that the good order, peace and security of the lives, liberty and property of the citizens should be maintained in the land, laws are enacted with penalties fixed for the punishment of those who commit crime against the citizens. It is necessary that the criminal should be brought before the bar of justice. It became my duty as an official of the State, appointed for such purpose, to see that the criminal should be brought before the bar, tried, and, if found guilty, pay the penalty attached to the crime. You are especially selected to hear the evidence, and after giving it consideration to say by your verdict whether the party charged with the crime· is guilty or not. Now, let us look back at the circumstances that bear upon this case, and see how they apply, and what weight should be given them in determining the guilt of the prisoner. In the first place, the justice before whom the first testimony was given judged it sufficient to hold him to answer before the grand jury. The grand jury investigated the case, and after hearing the evidence indicted him, and he is now

before you to answer for the crime of murder,
and on your verdict hangs his condemnation or
acquittal. Now there is always some strong
moving cause or motive on the part of the one
committing the crime, and impelling him to do
it. It is in proof that the prisoner and the
murdered man had been friends, had been together a great deal, and that the prisoner had
lost large amounts to him in play; that the
murdered man carried a large sum of money on
his person. Now, to regain this, the money he
had lost, and the possibility of getting much
more in addition, would have been a strong in-
ducement to the prisoner to commit the crime.
There may have been other motives.

"'The fact that the prisoner was last seen with
the murdered man near the Point of the Bluffs,
not far from which place the body was found,
the fact that the prisoner's knife was found not
far from the body, the fact that the prisoner was
absent from the village at the time, and his
utter refusal to account for his absence, point
strongly to the prisoner as the author of the
crime. No explanation of this is given. I cannot see how you can avoid reaching the conclusion that he is guilty of the crime as he is

charged in the indictment of the grand jury. If such testimony is not received to establish the guilt of criminals, few criminals would ever be punished for crime. Having confidence in your zeal to arrive at the truth in the case, and by your verdict to uphold the sanctity of the law, I submit the case to you, believing that you will do justice both to the prisoner and to the laws of your country.'

"After instructions by the court as to the law bearing on the case, the jury retired. After a short absence they returned the verdict, 'Not guilty,' and upon polling the jury each stated that to be his verdict."

A general shout was given by those in the court-room, and "Antoine received the congratulations of his many friends," as "The Herald" expressed it. Antoine saw Julie's white, agitated face in the crowd, but she disappeared without speaking to him.

CHAPTER XXXI.

CONFIDENCE.

THE months following Antoine's trial were full of sorrow. There was no improvement in Monsieur Beauvais' condition. Dr. Fisher came at regular intervals, not that he could benefit the Monsieur, but it was a comfort to Annette to see his kindly face, and to know that every attention was given to her father. The Doctor said one day, speaking of her to Monsieur St. Gemme:

"Other girls of her age are enjoying their pleasures in a selfish manner, peculiar to the young, who imagine that the earth was created for them. They never hear the refrain of sorrow and trouble that is constantly sent out. As people grow older that cry drowns all other sounds."

"Annette is not like other girls even in her pleasure," replied Monsieur St. Gemme.

"More is the pity, then, for when trouble comes

to such natures they absorb a double share, and
suffer in proportion."

"What is your opinion in regard to Monsieur
Beauvais?"

"He may last throughout the spring, or maybe for a longer time."

Monsieur St. Gemme dreaded the effect upon
Annette when the necessity of bearing up under
the strain was removed. Antoine seemed to
have something to worry him that was peculiarly
his own. He was estranged from his former
companions. "If Monsieur Beauvais dies, I do
not think Antoine will stay in Kaskaskia. In
that case, what will Annette do?" was a question
that proposed itself to Monsieur St. Gemme.

Antoine could not understand Louis' silence.
Leonie's fate he could only conjecture. Had
she received his letter before this accursed com-
bination of circumstances had closed in around
him? His father's condition was a continual
reproach to him. He felt that his course of
conduct had hastened the end. He wrote to
Louis a second time explaining the situation.
He told of the mysterious murder, the accusation,
his fidelity to his oath, and the shadow of suspicion that still rested on him.

"I would leave old 'Kaskia, but my father's precarious state forbids it. Louis, you must come or write. The Beauvais never desert a friend. I have been faithful to my vow, at what a fearful cost! Write and explain that I may be entirely exonerated in the mind of the public.

                                "Your friend,
                                        "ANTOINE."

Annette came into the room as he finished writing. His sad expression pained her beyond measure.

"Antoine," she said, "I fain would know what is in your heart. Why do you withhold your confidence from me? Every joy of yours was once mine, every grief of mine was yours."

"Annette," he said, "I am indeed unhappy. But you have enough to carry without my adding to your burden."

"No, no, Antoine, it were better that I know the cause of your unhappiness."

"Hear me, then. I am very much in debt. You are aware how foolishly I have wasted my time and money. I was led on by a vain hope that my luck would change next time, and I would play wildly to satisfy these delusions. But this hallucination, I trust, is broken forever." And he shuddered.

"But that is over now, Antoine."

He looked at her strangely. "Annette, do you not see?"—he arose and paced the floor rapidly —"the slightest breath of suspicion—it is unbearable. I, who would sacrifice everything for honor, to have dishonor heaped upon me! If it were not for poor papa, I would not remain here, but I cannot desert you, Annette—I am not base enough for that."

"Antoine, you have never been quite the same since you came back from Nouvelle Orleans."

"That is true. I have not. Annette," he continued hesitatingly, "I met and loved a pure young girl, for whom my whole soul calls out as does the traveler in the desert, perishing of thirst, yet knowing that in the distance, unattainable, is a spring of cool and delightful water. When in all confidence I sought her hand, her uncle, Monsieur Perrine, told me that she was destined for another, a handsome Spaniard—how I hated him!"

"What was the name of the young Ma'm'selle?"

"Leonie—Leonie de Villiers."

An indefinable feeling passed over Annette at this information. She and Antoine had been all in all to each other. Putting this aside, she gave her attention to what he was saying.

"I had a letter from Leonie last spring."

"Was she not then married?"

"No, she was not to be informed for another year. The time has gone by. When Monsieur Perrine's affairs became entangled, he, to save his credit, insisted that the marriage be consummated. Senor de Gonsalvo was the largest creditor, and would be satisfied with the hand of Leonie. I sent her a note, the day I left, promising to go to her assistance if she were in need of it at any time. Annette, you know how that promise has been kept. What scorn she must have for me. She will deem my excuse invented, and that I lack interest, or she may have changed. I am all in the dark. I have received no reply."

Annette tried to console Antoine as best she could.

During this conversation between brother and sister another was taking place in the kitchen. Rose was having an extra cleaning. Jule suddenly opened the door, "smiling with more than his usual impudence," as Rose called it.

"You, Jule, watch out dere! See dat puddle of water you 'bout to step into?"

"I'm in no wise particular, save for your sake, Madame Rose. It's a matter of no consequence."

Rose wondered what was coming, for Jule actually was forgetting the high-sounding French with which he usually tormented her.

"It am of great consequence if you step on dat floor dat is clean." And she threw out the window on its hinges, sprinkling the soap and water over him as she proceeded with the scrubbing.

Then he sobered down and said in a quiet voice: "Got company over to Madame Waring's."

"Humph," said Rose, "I didn't know dey was expecting company at dis time 'zactly."

"It's a young man, and come to stay."

"You, Jule," throwing the scrubbing-brush, which he dodged adroitly. It landed in the puddle and sent the drops splashing over the clean stones.

"Why couldn't you say in plain English dat Madame Waring got her son, and mighty proud she am, too?" And she relented, and laughed in her pleasure. "I must find out if Ma'm'selle hab heard dis." She picked her way through the debris of kettles and pans and hastened to find Annette.

"You have heard the news, Rose; I see it in your eyes," said Annette.   "I have just received a message from Madame Dubreil."

CHAPTER XXXII.

THE LAST CHANGE.

"ANTOINE," said Risden anxiously, "come quickly. There is some change in Monsieur. His eyes hab been roving restlessly about de room for de las' hour."

Risden had proved in this long illness of Monsieur Beauvais' that he had the rare faculty of the nurse, hence had been retained in the sickroom, and one of the slaves from the plantation had been brought to fill his place about the house. Annette was sitting by the side of the bed when Antoine entered.

"I think that papa wants something, Antoine. I cannot think what it may be. What is it, papa?" speaking to him softly, hoping that he might recognize her in some way. The sunken eyes were still for a moment, then began their restless search about the room, more often in the direction of the secretary. The Doctor had

hastily been summoned, and in a short time
Monsieur St. Gemme tapped lightly upon the
door. Antoine arose to admit him into the
apartments. "Papa is not the same," whispered
Annette as Monsieur St. Gemme stepped to her
side.

He saw that the last change was approaching.
"I think the priest would better be sent for," he
said.

Annette turned an affrighted look upon him.
"Is it so near?" she said brokenly.

"I am afraid so," he replied.

"Risden," said Antoine, "go."

The latter hurried to do Antoine's bidding.
He met the Doctor at the door. "You are going
for Father Olivier?" the latter said, divining
his object.

Risden bowed his head sadly.

"Doctor," said Annette, "papa seems to be
searching for something."

"What can it be?" asked the physician.
Suddenly Antoine crossed over to the secretary.
He had an indistinct recollection of seeing his
father, when he, Antoine, was but a little child,
take something out of a drawer. This, whatever
it was, the Monsieur had just as carefully re-

placed and locked within the drawer. Antoine opened the secretary, and, searching for the key for the inner drawer, found it, and soon discovered the miniature of a beautiful face, his mother's picture, which he placed reverently in his father's hand.

A light shot across the countenance of the sick man. He gazed at the beautiful features, and turned his eyes upward to heaven, as if he saw the original.

Father Olivier entered bearing the holy sacrament, which he administered to the dying man. The tired eyes closed wearily, never again to open on this world. His spirit was free to roam the celestial hills with the bride of his youth, to whose memory he had been so faithful all these years.

"It is all over," said the physician, and turned away.

"Come, Annette," said Monsieur St. Gemme, leading her from the room. Antoine's grief was violent and demonstrative, but Annette's silent, impassive demeanor alarmed St. Gemme.

"Annette," he cried, "Annette, you frighten me!"

She turned her dull eyes toward him. "He

was all I had," she said. "It was hard to see him go without one word for his children."

"Annette, your father has been lost to you for many months. Is not the release better for him than this 'death in life'?"

"He was my father," she answered in the same still way, and to Father Olivier, when he pronounced prayerful benedictions over her as he was leaving, the same dull glance was her only response.

"I will send Josephine and Madame Dubreil. They will know best what to do for her. Women know these things by instinct," thought St. Gemme. "Poor Monsieur Beauvais, I had not anticipated that such would be his end."

St. Gemme had felt a real affection for Monsieur Beauvais, and this had deepened as he saw that the elder man depended upon his judgment to such a degree.

The funeral service was attended by a large concourse of people. The assembly was doubtless augmented by numbers of the floating population, attracted by the peculiar and unfortunate turn of affairs in the family history.

The remains were taken to the consecrated ground adjoining the Church of the Immaculate

Conception, where the villagers had buried their dead these hundred years. Col. Menard supported the orphan daughter of his old friend. The slender young creature, in black attire, and heavily veiled, shuddered as she passed through the crowds, sensitive to the comments on such occasions. Antoine followed with Monsieur St. Gemme, Madame Dubreil with Josephine, and so the long procession was formed in order.

The solemn ritual for the dead fell in measured tones from the lips of the priest. He led to the grave, followed by the bearers. The entire assemblage knelt while the priest concluded the ceremony. The grave was sprinkled with holy water, and the thud of the clods was heard as the priest pronounced the words, "Earth to earth." Tears were in the eyes of all the villagers; sympathy was spontaneous and heart-felt in those days.

A few intimate friends accompanied the brother and sister to their desolate home. Madame Dubreil and Josephine were of the number. Madame Dubreil took Annette in charge. When she felt the hands of the young girl they were cold as ice.

"Annette, child, you are chilled." The girl

gave her a strange look. "You must have some warm drink at once." When this was brought she gave it to Annette. "Don't, Annette, don't look so!" cried Madame Dubreil, taking the girl into her arms, and holding her tight.

Annette broke into a wild spell of weeping. She sobbed and moaned piteously. Madame Dubreil placed her upon the couch, and when the first bitter agony was spent the bereaved girl fell into a deep sleep of exhaustion.

CHAPTER XXXIII.

THE FLIGHT.

It was the rich relative that relieved the situation at New Orleans. She had never fully recovered from the severe illness mentioned by Leonie to Antoine at their first meeting. Leonie still continued in high favor and made frequent visits to this relative.

One day shortly after Antoine's letter had been received, Leonie was very despondent. "Has Antoine become indifferent to me?" she thought. "Were his excuses sincere? No, I will believe in him." She said this over and over to herself, as if to sustain her waning courage.

Monsieur Perrine had informed her that very morning of the nuptials that were to take place on her approaching birthday.

"Come now, something grieves you," said her relative. "Has the bird died, or has Adele been cross with you in her tantrums, as she seems to think is her privilege?"

Leonie shook her head.

"What! none of these things? Then Senor de Gonsalvo is fickle and has neglected you at the ball."

"No, *cousine* Emilie. Do not speak of him," said Leonie with a frown.

"What, not hear of the Senor! What means all this? A handsome lover and grand, and his name must not be mentioned to you! Fie, fie upon thee!"

Leonie burst into tears.

"Leonie, Leonie, child. Tell me what is in your heart."

"*Cousine* Emilie, what shall I do? My uncle is determined that I shall marry the Senor, and I cannot, I cannot. I do not even like him."

"I do not like him myself," said the *cousine*. "But this is all new to me. Come, tell me more. Is there another my Leonie prefers?"

"*Cousine*," said Leonie, blushing and looking down, "when you were so ill, one night as Adele and I were going home at dusk, I slipped and fell. A young voyageur caught me and assisted me to rise."

At this hint of romance, the *cousine* rose to a sitting posture on her couch. "Go on," she said, impatiently.

"The next day, at dinner, you may judge of my surprise to meet the same young voyageur. He and Louis Vallé, my uncle's nephew, had come from a far distant point in the wilderness. I had often heard my uncle speak of these relatives."

"Never mind the relatives, but tell me of the young stranger."

"He recognized me immediately, as I did him. I saw it in one swift glance I gave to him. Then I looked down, for his eyes were full of admiration. Afterwards, in the garden, he referred to the previous meeting."

"Is that all?" asked the *cousine* in disappointed tones.

"No, I saw him frequently, and I know not how it happened, but—but—"

"But you two fell in love with each other. Ah, that is a breath of fresh air to me. What does Monsieur Perrine say?"

"He would not listen to Antoine."

"Antoine, is that the name of the fascinating youth?"

Leonie looked a little indignant at this remark, but merely answered: "Yes; Antoine—Antoine Beauvais."

"Ah, I knew his father. I cannot be mistaken. When we were neighbors in St. Pierre he left there, a broken-hearted man. But how did you know of the interview with Monsieur Perrine?"

"Antoine slipped a note into Adele's hand as he was leaving."

"Ah, young love laughs at bolts and bars, so I've heard," said the *cousine*, smiling. Then she looked grave and asked:

"What are young Beauvais' prospects in life?"

"I heard Louis Vallé say that old Monsieur Beauvais had large wealth, but I care not for that," she said naively. "Senor de Gonsalvo also has money and lands."

"Antoine your heart prefers, my Leonie."

A burning blush was the answer.

"They shall not marry you to the Senor. I have it. We shall outwit them." And Madame laughed. She had been a gay society belle, and was aroused at the thought of possible intrigue. "Leonie, I shall carry you away to France with me. Monsieur Perrine shall understand that you have relations on your father's as well as your mother's side."

Leonie gazed upon the *cousine* eagerly.

"Yes, my child, it occurs to me that I should

make that long promised visit to my *tante*. What say you? Your venerable *grandmere* will be delighted to see you."

Leonie appeared frightened at this, to her, great undertaking, but the *cousine* reassured her.

"You can have Adele bring a few things in a bag, between now and next Wednesday, for the vessel sails on that day, and we cannot risk a delay. Adele must bring you to say adieu to your dear *cousine* Emilie; you will accompany me on board the ship; you will neglect to return. I'll see to the Capitaine. I will care for you and protect you." She laughed slyly.

"But my uncle Perrine?" faltered Leonie.

"I shall invent an excuse which will make it necessary for him to go to the plantation on that day. We must get him up the river and away from the town."

"That will be very ungrateful to Monsieur Perrine."

Madame d'Arblay laughed merrily.

"But he will not mind that. He does not bid me Godspeed, for I am sadly out of his good graces. Now, Leonie, it is either this or stay and marry the Spaniard. It is you who must decide."

"That I will never do," she said with sudden vehemence.

"And, Leonie, *ma chere*,"—as she absently smoothed the folds of her silken wrapper, a ruffle of filmy lace failing over her delicate hands (she was very proud of her patrician hands),— "Tante Perrine must invite the Senor to drive with her on Wednesday." She smiled wickedly. "Monsieur Perrine will return; *tante* and the Senor will greet him, Leonie will be sent for, but, alas! the sweet bird will have flown."

Madame d'Arblay drew Leonie nearer, kissing lightly the eyes where the drops were still lingering on the lashes.

Madame did carry off the game before their very eyes.

"Leonie," she said when they were fairly out of the river, "I shall write from France that your *grandmere* wished to see you, and that is true, for who would not wish to see Leonie?"

Madame d'Arblay sighed as she thought of her own loveless match, and was resolved that Leonie should not have a like fate.

When they arrived at St. Pierre, they found Louis Vallé a guest at the Chateau de Villiers.

CHAPTER XXXIV.

LETTERS.

My dear Antoine:

"Your second letter has just reached me, and I am distressed beyond measure at the situation in which you are placed. I can only deplore my selfishness, which has brought this cloud upon you. I would not listen to Julie's better judgment, which said, 'Wait until my return.' I would not wait, for I thought life and maidens' hearts were uncertain. I have racked my brains to find a way out of this dilemma. Should *le grandpere* be apprised of the true situation just now, he would be more implacable than ever, by reason of this terrible result to you, in consequence of what he would call my rash act.

"Then, my Antoine, my most faithful friend, I entreat you to wait only a short time. I shall very soon be at liberty to return home, and I will at once make a clean breast of it to *le grandpere*. If he cuts me off it must be. I have one letter from Julie beside me. She relates her distress of mind during the time of your accusation and trial. The hermit of St. Anne's disappeared very suddenly the next week after our marriage was performed. She knew not what course to pursue, but she writes: 'I went to the trial fully determined in my own mind, if the result was against Antoine, to then declare the reason of his silence respecting his absence from the village. No harm must come to Antoine.'

"I have news for you. Leonie is here at the chateau. Madame d'Arblay, a cousin of Leonie's mother, made a successful *coup d'etat*, and brought Leonie away with her. Madame d'Arblay is not fond of Monsieur Perrine. He sneers at her invalid ideas, and Madame will not forgive that. Madame and I have won the *grandmere* over to our side.

"By the way, Madame is a very graceful woman. She was a great belle in her youth, so *le grandmere* says.

"Adieu, then, until I see you, my noble friend.

"I am faithfully yours,

"LOUIS VALLE."

This letter was received late in the summer. Matters were unsettled with the brother and sister. No change had been made, but Antoine was restless, as Annette could plainly see. He took this letter to Annette with shining eyes.

She read it and then said abruptly: "You are going?"

He looked grave and said: "Not without you, Annette. We will both go."

"No, Antoine. I wish not to cross the sea. If you go it must be alone," she said decidedly.

"Shall I desert you?" he replied; "do you suppose me to be heartless?"

"But if I do not wish to go?" she answered.

"What is in your heart?"

This was always the form of asking confidence.

"Marie tells me that Monsieur Waring wishes to lease the Beauvais house. She wishes me to make my home with them, but I would not have it so. I have thought to go east to the convent of Our Ladies of the Visitation."

"Annette, not that," Antoine cried in surprised tones. "You have not weighed the matter carefully. You would not forsake the world. You do not know it yet. A home and an honored husband should be your portion."

"That is not for me," she said quietly, her large eyes fixed steadily on his.

Antoine did not speak. This was a new thought to him. He supposed Annette's resolve was due to sorrow for their father's death, and that in time she would relinquish the idea. His own heart just then was full of a sweet hope. His nature was naturally buoyant, and he began to plan a future whose brightness should atone

for the gloom of the past. He saddened only at
the thought that his father would not be with
him to witness this joy.

Antoine replied to Louis' letter, saying that
he would join him at St. Pierre, and asking Louis
to await is coming.

.   .   .   .   .   . "Our home is desolate since
the dear father is gone. Neither Annette nor I
care to remain where everything reminds us of
his presence. Annette will either decide to accompany me to France or go to the sisters at
Georgetown. Ma'm'selle Somers has inclina-
tion to return to her English home next month.
Annette suggests that we go with her as far as
our course is in the same direction.

"Louis, what entanglements we weave around
each other when we strive to carry out our individual designs! Sometimes I think, 'Why strive,
why almost sell our souls to gain the thing that
is in our heart, that desire calls for? Eternity
is at our door, this life is naught, sit still and
wait for the next.' And yet, when the new
blood courses through our veins, we simply repeat ourselves; the same plans, the same keen
desires, the same restless seeking absorb us from
day to day. Adieu, dear Louis.

"ANTOINE BEAUVAIS."

Some weeks later Antoine and Annette were
on their way to Vincennes, where they would

meet one of the five daily coaches that ran on the "National Road." The Warings had taken possession of the Beauvais mansion until brother and sister might wish to reclaim it.

"Marie," said Annette, "we will leave Risden and Rose in your care. You will, I know, be kind to them."

Waring and Monsieur St. Gemme were to look after the large estate. Antoine never troubled himself about business matters. Monsieur Beauvais had not trained him to such exertion. "The Americans that had lately come could push the enterprises of the village if they chose." Annette, of course, was ignorant in respect to such things.

CHAPTER XXXV.

"ANNETTE, I cannot think your purpose is fixed," Antoine had said to her. "I need you now; come with me. What if— " He could not finish the sentence.

"I will humor him for the present," Annette resolved.

Antoine believed that, if Annette would travel, in the end she would change her mind, but she said to herself: "What is there in life for me but to devote myself to the church, and there find a refuge from this unrest in my soul?"

When they arrived at St. Pierre, their relatives received them as if they had been denizens of another world. France and St. Pierre were real to the brother and sister, but to their friends the wilderness was but a vague conception.

Louis had awaited them eagerly. As was the fashion, he kissed Antoine on either cheek and grasped his hands as if never to release them.

268

"Antoine, thou faithful one," he cried.

"Never mind, Louis. It is past now. Time will set all right." But nevertheless a sad look passed over his face at the recollection. "But tell me—Leonie?"

"She is here."

A door opened, and Leonie stood before them. Louis wisely deemed his presence unnecessary and withdrew. What passed at that interview may be inferred.

Antoine was duly presented to *la grandmere*, and he must have made a favorable impression, for early the next spring, when the air was bright with sunshine, and the flowers were in bloom, and the birds singing, the nuptials of Antoine and Leonie took place in the same chapel where his father had so proudly wed a young bride.

Annette rejoiced in Antoine's happiness, and, though both he and Leonie were kind and loving in their efforts to make her life also bright, she could not feel at home in this new life. She often roamed about the places where her mother's girlhood had been spent. Monsieur Beauvais' oft-told description had made every nook familiar to her.

As time passed on, there were many suitors

for the hand of the "beautiful Ma'm'selle Beauvais, who had lived where the Indians were her
neighbors." Antoine wondered at her indifference. It was contrary to established custom.
"Annette should marry as was proper for all girls
to do in France."

Annette wrote to Marie in one of the occasional letters that passed between them:

"I knew not how strongly the fibers of my
heart were entwined about old 'Kaskia. I miss
it every day. I do not seem to fit in with the
life here. I miss the sound of our old bell at
home calling me to early mass. When I look
out of my window the first thing in the morning, I do not see the sun peeping over the old
fort on Garrison Hill, his beams touching the
mists arising from the river, and changing the
gray to white, the patches of bluffs showing as
islands in a sea of foam. I miss the song of the
voyageurs, the crooning of the slaves at their
labor. I miss the crack of the rifle, with its
resounding echoes among the hills, when the
couriers du bois are chasing their game. I miss
my light-hearted Marie, and how sadly I miss
the dear papa and the old home."

Marie did not hear from Annette for a number
of months after this letter was received. A report came in a roundabout way through some
friends who had been in Nouvelle Orleans that

Annette had married into a family of rank, that her husband was an officer in the French army. This was generally believed, but Marie wondered at Annette's silence.

Louis Vallé had a stormy interview with *le grandpere.* The old gentleman would not listen to reason, but Louis patiently waited until the first effect had subsided, when he argued that the deed was done; that if his grandfather pursued the course with which he threatened him, then was Antoine's sacrifice in vain.

"Louis," said *le grandpere,* brokenly, "I had my plans for you, lad."

"I know, *grandpere,* but the heart dictates—"

"Leave me now," said *le grandpere.*

In the end Louis triumphed, and was reinstated in favor.

Madame Dubreil had occasion to make a second trip in regard to her estates. She decided to dispose of them and invest the amount in and about the village. She brought Annette back with her.

"I think, child," she said, "the sight of your old home is what you need. Come with me."

When again they found themselves in dear old 'Kaskia, Marie met them with the word that

Josephine had been taken with sudden conges-
tion, and had been buried the previous month.
Monsieur St. Gemme had gone to the Rocky
Mountains to take charge of Menard & Vallé's
business.   Henri was with him.

THE KASKASKIA HOTEL.

CHAPTER XXXVI.

LAFAYETTE'S VISIT.

THE village was all excitement. Every one was in holiday attire. The preparations were completed to receive the Marquis de Lafayette in the best style that the village afforded. Gen. Edgar would entertain him, the banquet would be held at the old tavern, and a ball at night in the grand stone house of William Morrison. All the finery possessed by the dames and young maids would be brought to light.

At an early hour the streets were filled with animated groups. Foot travelers, horsemen and charettes were pouring in from the country far and near. The young men who were to form the guard of honor were dashing back and forth on prancing horses. Old women in linsey, with blue handkerchiefs on their heads; young ones in print (then a luxury), with gay Madras handkerchiefs at throat; men in hunting outfit of dressed deer-skin; Indians in blankets—a motley crowd.

As the guard of honor made another dash, Marie said:

"See young Savinian Delusiere (St. Vrain); does he not look fine to-day, Annette?"

The two were watching the passers-by.

"Ah, there is Col. Menard; his silk hat has an extra brushing for the occasion."

"What are he and Father Olivier discussing so earnestly?"

"I don't know," said Annette, absently. "Perhaps who will sit at the right hand of the Marquis at the banquet."

"Ah, there comes Monsieur Waring," said Marie, as her husband galloped by, throwing a kiss to the two at the window. "Louis Buyatte is out. I should think it a geat risk at his age."

"He wishes to be part of it once more," Annette said. "I wonder how it would seem to be as old as he."

"See Moqua and old Francoise. She carries her last basket. Is she going to give it to Lafayette?" laughed Marie. "There go the young men again. Ah, they are now at Menard & Vallé's store. No, I am mistaken. Col. Menard is giving them instructions merely. I know that they are impatient to be off. Gen. Edgar looks *distingué* in his uniform. Did you see that portrait of him standing by the side of his white charger?"

"Yes. Look, Marie, they are sending in the cakes for the banquet. Madame Godin cannot be excelled in her pound-cake. Poor papa used to say there was nothing like it this side of France."

"What is the *menu?*"

"Cold turkey and chicken for Madame, and roast pig for Monsieur, the most delicious cakes that can be made by the 'Kaskia *chef*, plates of toothsome nothings—I cannot tell it all, Marie. French coffee, of course."

"We will go later and have a glimpse at the tables."

"Let us go into the street."

"Wait a little moment." Marie must again kiss the sleeping *enfant*.

Bright, expectant faces were on every corner. A laugh, a *bon mot*, a greeting of friends and acquaintances. Old men were relating, to all that would listen, incidents of the war of '76—Lafayette's bravery, his valor, his generosity, his kindness of heart, his patriotism. And then the talk would drift to the more recent Indian wars.

Deeds of courageous daring or of successful
strategy in dealing with the red man were told
with great zest.

The arches were being covered with roses. One
placed opposite to the gate of the Maxwell home
was especially beautiful.

"See," said Madame Odile, holding up a *bou-
tonniere*. "These are buds of the Damask rose-
bush grown from a slip brought from France.
They are for the Marquis."

Marie nodded approvingly.

"Foster has taken a large basketful of roses to
the banquet-room," Madame Odile continued.
"There is to be a rainbow of flowers to span
the table at which the Marquis will sit."

"Are the laurel wreaths in place yet?" asked
Annette.

"Yes, the decorations are about completed."

"Isn't it beautiful! I wish a marquis would
come very day of the year except Sunday," said
Marie childishly.

"Fie, fie," said Annette.

"Let us watch the young men form." And
with laughing adieux they followed the crowd
past the old State-house. The narrow streets
were jammed. The guard of honor started off

in grand style at the head of the procession.

"Come," said Marie, "a peep at the tables, and then home to prepare for the reception."

The cheers of the villagers announced the approach of Lafayette and the distinguished people from St. Louis and other places, as well as the leading citizens of old 'Kaskia. There was an equally excited crowd awaiting the arrival, and strewing roses before the approaching guest. Gen. Edgar's mansion, the resort of the fashionable society of the country, was thrown open to the company.

Gov. Coles delivered the address of welcome on behalf of the people of Illinois. The Marquis responded in a most feeling manner.

The crowd made way for a group of veterans, some of whom Lafayette recognized as having fought under him at Brandywine and Yorktown. This was a most affecting scene. The scars of hard-fought battles called out the involuntary respect of the spectators.

Lafayette gazed on them with pride and affection beaming in his eyes. Were not they the champions of the cause he loved so well? He himself was slightly lame from a wound in the same service.

"Is he not grand?" whispered Marie. They had taken position at an angle of the gallery. "See the color of his coat—maroon—and gold lace trimmings."

"Hush, Marie," said Annette.

After the ceremonies the spirits of the people began to lighten. The formalities had been properly observed, and now the festivities were to open. The banquet was ready, and Lafayette was escorted to the place of honor at the rainbow table. The large room of the tavern was a bower. Col. Menard sat at the Marquis' right hand, and Father Olivier at the left. Grace was said, the covers lifted, and the feast was before them. Hearts were happy, tongues were unloosed, and time was forgotten. Then followed the toasts.

Gov. Coles, bowing to the Marquis, said earnestly, "The inmates of La Grange, let them not be uneasy. Though their father is one thousand miles in the interior of America, he is yet in the midst of his affectionate children."

Lafayette's son, George Washington Lafayette: "The grateful confidence of my father's children and grandchildren in the kindness of his American family toward him."

The Marquis offered the following toast: "Kaskaskia and Illinois—may their joint prosperity more and more evince the blessings of congenial industry and freedom."

Gov. Bond's toast: "Gen. Lafayette—may he live to see that liberty established in his native country which he helped to establish in his adopted country."

"Sir," said Lafayette, "in reference to the latter part of your toast, I must drink that standing."

This sentiment met with sympathetic applause on the part of the listeners.

But the great ball at William Morrison's. The servants were running hither and thither, putting finishing touches to rooms already beautiful. The dancing was to be in the large upper apartment, and refreshments were to be served on the lower floor. An elegant collation was served on this very eventful occasion. Foster was on hand, and many a hint was volunteered by her as to "how dey did at Nouvelle Orleans at de Jackson banquet." This made the other servants stare. The matrons came early in order to see the arrivals.

"Ah, here comes Madame Rozier. How elegant she is in the new costume," said one.

"Ah, I must speak with Monsieur Le Brun. Here is an opportunity to inquire after my cousin in St. Louis," said another.

"Ah," said Madame La Chappelle, "there is Delusiere with Virginia Menard, the Colonel's niece," as the young guard passed with a small dark-haired girl on his arm. "No handsomer couple will be here to-night."

"They are all beautiful, beautiful," said Madame Derousse. "Come, Annette and Marie, come, that I may tell you how lovely you both are."

Marie smiled saucily, but Annette was indifferent. She was dressed in a rich brocade that had been her mother's—wine background with masses of flowers over it. Some pearls were woven in the coils of her magnificent hair; a brooch that was an heirloom fastened the lace of her bodice. Her large eyes were aglow, and a slight flush upon the creamy skin. The pulses of a rich, warm life were running in her veins. An occasion of this kind seemed to fill out the measure of her being.

"The party from Col. Menard's are soon to arrive. Gen. and Mrs. Edgar are here, and they are expecting the others to arrive every moment," said Waring.

THE LAFAYETTE BANQUET ROOM.—KASKASKIA HOTEL.

FROM A PHOTO IN 1893.

"Ah, here they come."

Lafayette was with Col. Menard and Madame. They were accompanied by the Choteaus, the Gratiots, the Vallés and others of the visitors. They formed a group about William Morrison and his family. Madame Odile Maxwell and her sister, Alzire Menard, were in this group.

"See," the whispers passed around the room, "the Marquis is going to open the ball with Alzire Menard."

As he led forth the young girl, who was a noted belle, a murmur of admiration was heard. Alzire wore a beautiful new gown of peach-blossom silk that had been made expressly for the ball.

Other couples wheeled into line, and the graceful movements of the ladies and the stately dignity of their escorts made an impression never to be forgotten. In fact the ball at William Morrison's, "when Lafayette was here," was a favorite topic with the villagers long afterwards, when not a stone was left to mark the spot where stood the spacious mansion.

"Who is that handsome Ma'm'selle sitting by Madame Dubreil?" asked George Kenerly, a desirable *parti* from St. Louis.

"That is Annette Beauvais. A sad history connected with her, but she bore it nobly."

"I should like to be presented."

Kenerly asked Ma'm'selle for the honor of the next dance. This happened to be the "Co-quette," a favorite movement with the Kaskas-kians. Alzire Menard was led out into the same set. It was rumored that Alzire was a greater attraction than the Marquis in bringing Kenerly to 'Kaskia at this time. Delusiere and Virginia Menard made another couple.

"A galaxy of stars," exclaimed Monsieur Jar-rot, one of the honored guests. "Who is the stately Ma'm'selle with Kenerly?"

"Old Monsieur Beauvais' daughter, you understand."

"Ah, yes. Her brother is in France, you say?"

"Yes, for some years."

"Where does Ma'm'selle Beauvais make her home these days?"

"With Marie—Madame Waring. They were friends from childhood."

"What became of the property? There was a large fortune, was there not?"

"Antoine has the estate, but Annette is well

provided for in the way of investments that are becoming more valuable as the country advances. She will probably return to France, so I hear."

"But what is the stir about the Marquis?" And the two keen traders leave off their business speculation and hasten to the scene of interest.

"Marquis, there is an Indian woman, Sciakape, who insists upon seeing you, and will not be put off."

"What is her desire?"

"She has a paper that she wishes to show."

"We must inquire into the matter."

"Will the great white father look at Sciakape and have patience with her?"

"What is it, my child?"

The daughter of a chief, Paneiciowa, of the Six Nations, stood before him.

"My father, a great chief, the white father a great chief, my father say, and he fight and make war too, and my father fight, see." And she handed him a paper, soiled and worn, in Lafayette's own writing. "This he gave me when he died. I am to keep it always, never let go."

"Yes. I gave this to your father for his valor. He was a great chief, a brave warrior."

Sciakape looked pleased at this.

"I hear a great way off that you were the white chief. I start at this first light, when the stars go back in the sky. Some of my people come too. We ride far."

Lafayette was touched at this—the memory of himself hidden away all these years in the heart of the red man and made sacred to his child and to his people. With appropriate words and gifts, he praised Sciakape for so carefully treasuring this testimony of her father. When he returned to the gay scene, his heart was full of emotion at this new proof of the affection felt for him in this great America that he had helped to perpetuate.

At midnight Lafayette and his suite were escorted to the landing, but the dancers did not disperse until morning.

"Marie," said Annette, "Gen. Lafayette has come and gone and our 'to-morrow of anticipation' is a thing of the past."

CHAPTER XXXVII.

IL PARAIT.

For months the talk of the village was upon Lafayette's visit, the ball, the banquet, the strangers who had come to celebrate the occasion. That he had come eight hundred miles out of his way to do honor to old 'Kaskia was a matter of pride with them. If perchance a single individual could be found who, for some reason, had not been present, what an opportunity for minute description of each and every detail; and what bitter pangs of regret assailed the absentees when the festivities were mentioned.

It was late in the summer when Waring announced that word had been received fom St. Gemme, and that he would arrive in October. Marie was voluble in her expressions of joy that his life had been preserved during the two years he had been with the wild Indians of the Rockies.

Annette was silent. The name brought back

the past vividly—the time of trouble and great sorrow, when he had been so closely connected with the interests of her life. Would he have changed in these years? What was she expecting? She started and scorned herself for the thought. How utterly baseless were such conjectures. He had always been kind to her, but that was his nature, to be considerate of others.

Marie each day had some new anecdote to relate of the children, their growth—it was marvelous. And the husband, Edgar Waring, there must be this and that done for his comfort and well-being.

"Marie, who would have thought you would become so domestic—the giddy creature that you were before you met Monsieur, your husband?"

Marie gazed earnestly at Annette. Her figure had still its old grace, but the sparkle in her eyes was more subdued. "I am very happy, Annette. My life is full of the joy of my home and my family. I wish, Annette, the same joys were yours."

An unspeakable depth of pain was in the dark eyes that Annette turned to Marie. "Don't, Marie. My path has led me by these things."

It was the evening of the same day that Annette was irresistibly led to seek her father's grave. The conversation with Marie had aroused a melancholy train of memories. The old-time longing and reaching-out for something that her nature claimed, which had been denied, was again upon her.

The sun had set in a glow of crimson and gold, a purple haze covering the hills on the east side of the river. But the radiance had departed, and a gray mist began to settle over the valley. Annette was leaning against the slab that marked her father's grave. "Ah, papa," she murmured, "I understand the great solitude that was in your heart those long years. An utter loneliness of spirit into which neither the world nor thy children could enter. I am a woman now and I know the desolation."

A figure had stolen around the corner of the old church, and for a few seconds was motionless. It was Monsieur St. Gemme. He knelt by the side of the girl, unconscious of his presence, and drew her closely to his side.

"Annette, God is good; he has permitted me once more to gaze on thy dear face."

She remained silent.

"Annette, is all my love and devotion in vain?

God knows how sorely my heart cries out for you
—how the thought of this moment has borne
me up when else I would have perished under
privation. and suffering.   Again and again has it
nerved me to make one more effort to reach you.
Tell me the truth, Annette."

"Monsieur, I cannot remember the time when
I have not loved and trusted you.   Your image
has filled my heart when it was a sin to think of
you.   I even thought to take the veil that I
might overcome and conquer—"

"The lonely heart shall have rest," he murmured, and he pressed his lips to hers in ecstasy.
Crossing himself, he said: "As God in Heaven
hears me, may I ever be true and faithful to
Annette, daughter of my loved and honored
friend, the Monsieur Beauvais St. Pierre."

They rose to their feet and with hushed voices
left the consecrated ground.   On the way home
he told her how he had lost the trail, and of his
capture by hostile Indians, who had subjected
him and his companions to cruel tortures.   He and
others had succeeded in making their escape.
It would have been sure death to remain in the
Indian village.   Another prisoner was a Dela-
ware Indian to whom St. Gemme had by acci-

RUINS OF THE OLD CONVENT.—Kaskaskia.

dent rendered a favor. This Indian sickened and died, but he gave to St. Gemme an old belt and leather wallet on the inside of which was stamped in ink, "C. Le Fevre," and confessed to having murdered a pale-face not far from the village of Kaskaskia.

"Annette," said St. Gemme, showing them to her, "this forever exonerates Antoine from a shadow of doubt."

A light was in her face as she listened.

"Antoine, brother," she exclaimed, "that you could know, even as I do hear, this strange tale!"

St. Gemme and Annette were quietly married at the mansion the following month. "In great sorrow or in great happiness I can bear only my nearest to be with me," said Annette.

The Warings built a home on the banks of the river, and Annette was again established in the "Beauvais Mansion," with the familiar faces of Risden and Rose about her.

CHAPTER XXXVIII.

THE FLOOD OF '44.

TWENTY years have rolled away—years in which the villagers have feasted and fasted, have married and departed this life, as they had been doing for a century or more. The American population had rapidly increased during this time. Settlements to the east and to the south were dividing the attention, but still old 'Kaskia contained the wealth and fashion of this section. Edgar Waring was a leading man in politics. He had grown wealthy by judicious business investments. Marie was always the same bright creature. Annette's powers had ripened with the years. As Col. Menard predicted, she was "a queen among women." The happiness of which she had dreamed when a girl had been hers. She had found the meaning in life, through the channel of a complete and absorbing devotion to her husband. The refined intelligence of Monsieur St. Gemme, his delicate tact, his far-reaching knowledge of men and affairs, his varied experience gained by traversing large tracts of country in early life, in contact both with the civilized and the savage, gave him a charm and fascination of character that gratified her pride. Their home was the resort of all the intelligence and culture that the West then afforded. Education had made an advance in these years. Several sisters from Georgetown had established a convent in the building celebrated by the banquet to Lafayette. But Col. Menard, with his accustomed liberality, had out of his princely fortune built a handsome four-story brick structure known as the Convent of "Our Lady of the Visitation."

Annette's youngest daughter, a fairy-like little creature, is to be one of the May queens at the coming exhibitions in May. Sister Ellen and Sister Josephine are training the girls for the important event.

But the rains are frequent this spring. The March rise is unprecedented. In April the water threatens the village. But the people are concerned for another reason. Old Col. Menard, whom every one loves, is failing, is ill. "Has he not helped all when in distress? Does he not

keep half the people?   No one applies for help
and is refused."

Still the water is coming up slowly.

"Monsieur, I think the little Angelique" (named
for the Colonel's wife) should be brought home."

"Ah, not yet, Annette.   There is time," said
Monsieur St. Gemme.

The water is in the streets.

"Monsieur, I shall send for the little Angelique."

"Yes, now, if you wish."

Rose is sent to the convent.

Rose is old, but no older than in the time of
Monsieur Beauvais.

Angelique will not go with Rose.

"What, Rose, would mamma wish me to miss
being the May queen?   Tell her I love her, but
I shall have to stay."   And she cried so that
Sister Ellen would not force her.

Rose is sent three times for the small Angelique, who finally is carried off on Rose's back,
screaming down the street.

"The Madame say I bring you dis time sure,"
said Rose.

The waters are rising faster.   The great June
rise is here.   The water is up to the sills; a

few more inches, and then in the door. The
houses nearest the river are deserted.

"I say we are going to have Noah's flood,"
said old Madame Latulippe. "The people are
wicked, and they play and dissipate. They will
not listen to Father St. Cyr when he reproves
them. We shall all perish, all perish." And
she rocked back and forth.

"No, no," said Basyl Taumur.

"I say it. Father St. Cyr was seen on the
top of Garrison Hill, standing by the old fort
with his hands spread out toward old 'Kaskia,
and he cursed us with this great flood. Toinette
said it. We all shall perish—shall perish."

The word is passed around that Col. Menard
is lying very low. "Col. Menard is dead." The
whole village mourn as one family, when, on the
9th of June, the remains are brought to the
village for burial.

The ferry passes from the door of his mansion
to the Kaskaskia Hotel, over the sea of water.
Father Donatien St. Cyr and his choristers,
as a mark of especial honor, meet the bier at
this place, from whence the large assemblage of
people follow to the church for the last solemn
service.

The water is still rising; the people have fled to the bluffs on the east side. The water is everywhere, even back to the hills, where stands the old mill.

The steamer Indiana is taking the nuns out of the second story. Many of the villagers boarded that boat to never again return to 'Kaskia. Among the number were Edgar Waring and Marie. Monsieur St. Gemme and Annette are on the brow of the bluff, gazing upon the wild waste beneath them.

Annette is leaning against the old tree at whose base she had sat long years ago. The same far-away look is in her eyes.

"What is it, my wife, my beloved? What do you see?"

She turned to him with a luminous face. "France and my brother Antoine."

"So it shall be, Annette."

Hand in hand they walk down the precipitous path. The years ever bring these two natures into truer unison.

When the waters subside, there are entire streets upon which are left only the tall chimneys to mark the place where homes had once existed. A new era has set in—one of decay, and a gradual disappearance of the villagers.

Never again will be the glory of the "Old 'Kaskia Days."

THE END.

www.ingramcontent.com/pod-product-compliance
Lightning Source LLC
Chambersburg PA
CBHW030933260626
47169CB00002B/458